The Baldasseri Royals

Destined to rule...*and* live happily ever after?

Welcome to San Vantino...home to siblings
Prince Rini, Prince Vincenzo and
Princess Bella Baldasseri. The family
may appear to live a charmed life—they're
royalty, after all!—but that doesn't mean
that every day is plain sailing.

Now they must face their greatest challenge.
Can they devote themselves to their kingdom
and let themselves find true love? Well...we're
about to find out!

Step inside the palace with...

Rini and Luna's story
Reclaiming the Prince's Heart

Vincenzo and Francesco's story
Falling for the Baldasseri Prince

and

Bella and Luca's story
Second Chance with His Princess
Available now!

Dear Reader,

When I was a little girl, my dear grandmother received what we all called the gold book. It was a gift from a friend who'd been to the Golden Jubilee in London. There were pictures of the royal family, of Elizabeth and Margaret when they were little girls. I loved that book and went through it all the time, looking at the crown jewels and the castles, the horses and pets, and the royal family draped in ermine for royal photographs. As I grew up, I followed the story of Queen Elizabeth and her marriage and her children. I was fascinated until the death of Princess Diana. Then stories came out about the family and their problems, and they saddened me.

This last year I've thought a lot about being born into a royal family and the hardships one might have to endure. I finally decided to write my trilogy about the Baldasseri royal family. The first book shows problems with the crown prince developing amnesia. The second shows the difficulties of a royal son having to carry out his royal duty when his heart lies elsewhere. Now this third novel tells of a princess who loves a commoner.

Enjoy!

Rebecca Winters

Second Chance with His Princess

Rebecca Winters

Recycling programs
for this product may
not exist in your area.

ISBN-13: 978-1-335-40711-5

Second Chance with His Princess

Copyright © 2022 by Rebecca Winters

For questions and comments about the quality of this book, please contact us at CustomerService@Harlequin.com.

Harlequin Enterprises ULC
22 Adelaide St. West, 41st Floor
Toronto, Ontario M5H 4E3, Canada
www.Harlequin.com

Printed in U.S.A.

Rebecca Winters lives in Salt Lake City, Utah. With canyons and high alpine meadows full of wildflowers, she never runs out of places to explore. They, plus her favorite vacation spots in Europe, often end up as backgrounds for her romance novels—because writing is her passion, along with her family and church. Rebecca loves to hear from readers. If you wish to email her, please visit her website at rebeccawinters.net.

Books by Rebecca Winters

Harlequin Romance

The Baldasseri Royals

Reclaiming the Prince's Heart
Falling for the Baldasseri Prince

Secrets of a Billionaire

The Greek's Secret Heir
Unmasking the Secret Prince

Escape to Provence

Falling for Her French Tycoon
Falling for His Unlikely Cinderella

The Princess Brides

The Prince's Forbidden Bride
How to Propose to a Princess

Visit the Author Profile page at Harlequin.com for more titles.

I've dedicated this novel to my dearest, sweetest nana, Alice Vivia Driggs Brown, my beloved father's mother. She was an angel in my life and taught me everything, from the Bible stories to the stories of kings. I can't wait to see her again one day and let her know how much she enriched my life!

Praise for
Rebecca Winters

"This is the first book that I have read by this author but definitely not the last as it is an amazing story. I definitely recommend this book as it is so well written and definitely worth reading."

—*Goodreads* on *How to Propose to a Princess*

PROLOGUE

*Scuol, Graubunden Canton,
Switzerland, the end of April*

THE LAST FRIDAY morning announcement came over the high school's PA system. "Hey, all you ski bums—don't forget when the bell rings in a few minutes, come straight out to the back of the school where the bus is waiting. We want to get up on the mountain fast before the sun makes things slushy."

Just the sound of Luca Torriani's deep voice excited sixteen-year-old Bella Baldasseri to her core. Not only was he a brilliant student, he was president of their school and ski club. His expertise on the slopes had caught the attention of the ski world. Already becoming famous at eighteen, he'd won a place on the Swiss men's ski team to train for the Olympics.

Luca had been her brother Vincenzo's best friend for as long as she could remember. Over the years he'd been a constant visitor to the palace. She'd spent most of her free time with them, preferring to be with dark-haired Luca more than any guy alive. In truth, she loved him heart and soul. There would never be anyone else for her. *Not ever.*

"Bella? Can I sit on the bus with you?" Deep in thoughts about him, her friend Margite's question startled her. She hadn't noticed the bell had rung, but the students were running around. Bella had hopes that when Luca came on board, he'd sit by her. But she couldn't say no to her friend. Margite had a hopeless crush on Vincenzo.

"Sure. We've got to hurry and grab our skis." Like Margite, she was already dressed in ski clothes. Before long they took their equipment outside in back where the driver loaded their gear on the side of the bus. She deliberately chose a seat near the back where she knew her brother and Luca liked to sit.

The bus filled up fast and soon she spotted the two of them coming down the aisle, talking to everybody. When Luca drew close, his emerald eyes fastened on her. They looked like the green in the stained-glass windows going up the stairs to her room. She was mesmerized by the way they penetrated.

"'Is the Princess ready to tackle Devil's Gulch?"

She winced, wishing he wouldn't call her Princess. Bella wanted him to think of her as an ordinary girl like all the others. "Just watch me."

"I plan to." His dashing smile got to her before he moved to the back seat. Her brother greeted Margite, but he kept going.

Twenty minutes later they'd arrived at the ski resort and climbed out under a full sun, ready to tackle the slopes. To her joy, Luca pulled his skis and hers off the rack. Together they put them on. "This is going to be fun," she said as he handed her the poles she'd brought. Slipping on goggles and a helmet over her jaw-length hair, she was ready.

Luca pulled on his gloves. "All right, let's

push off so you can show me your latest technique." She chuckled because she didn't have one and he knew it.

Her brother had been distracted by some guys and didn't join them. That was an answer to prayer. Bella was dying to be alone with Luca. Every feminine eye was envious as they struck out for the Devil's Gulch trail.

To her surprise a sign had been erected she hadn't seen all winter. *Danger of avalanche.* No one else would try it now, but she would prove to be the exception. "Are you game?" She looked back at him, daring him.

He studied her through narrowed eyes, as if trying to see inside her. "It's not safe. Let's ski Bishop's Cauldron."

"I prefer the Gulch." She knew he favored it too. In the next breath she took off and shushed down the trail.

"Bella—" he shouted. "Stop and come back here!"

"You'll have to catch me!" She laughed, confident in her own abilities.

She'd been skiing with Vincenzo and Luca since she was nine and knew this mountain well. Now that spring had come, the snow was heavier, but just as divine as always. Her euphoria knew no bounds as he came after her.

To know that the great Luca Torriani was chasing her made Bella's mad dash down the face ten times more exhilarating. Seconds later she heard an ear-splitting crack from above. The ground trembled beneath her skis. "Bella!" he shouted at the top of his lungs. *"Avalanche!"*

She slowed to a stop and looked up in time to see a chute of snow full of trees cascading from the summit. Luca reached her and pulled her down to remove her skis and his. "We can't outrun this avalanche, Bella. When it covers us, try to swim up and out of it. Don't forget to raise your arms."

It was getting closer. She grabbed onto him. "If we're going to die, I'm thankful I'm with you. I love you, Luca."

He pulled her close and kissed her mouth. "I love you, too, Bella. Always will. Brace yourself. Here it comes!"

Snow filled her nostrils like dust. She felt herself being buried. "Luca—" she screamed before she couldn't breathe.

The next time she had cognizance of her surroundings, it was night. She'd awakened in the hospital in Scuol with an IV in her arm. "Luca? Luca?"

"No, darling. You're awake, thank heaven." Her mother stood at the side of the hospital bed with a pallor she'd never seen before.

"Don't look so worried, Mamma. I feel fine."

"It's a miracle you escaped without injury."

"That's because of Luca."

Her mother leaned over her. "We've been waiting for you to fully awaken. The doctor says you can go home in the morning. Your father is out in the hall with him."

"Where's Vincenzo?"

"Leonardo asked him to fly to San Vitano on a special assignment. I don't know how long he'll be gone. The doctor wants to keep you here overnight just to be certain there are no compli—"

"How's Luca?" she interrupted her. He was all she cared about now that she was conscious. "Please tell me he wasn't injured. I couldn't bear it if—"

"He's alive," her mother responded. "He was in surgery all afternoon."

All afternoon? She'd lost hours. "What happened to him? Tell me!"

"It's his right leg. A snapped tree slammed into him, but the search and rescue teams got to the two of you in record time. You were airlifted here."

Bella groaned, wanting to die. "Do you think he'll be able to ski again?"

"No." The news dropped like a bomb, horrifying her. "But the doctor believes he might be able to walk."

"Might?" Filled with gut-wrenching guilt and pain, Bella buried her face in the pillow. "Luca warned me not to go down the Gulch. He tried to stop me. When I kept going, it forced him to follow me." Bella started sobbing. "It's my fault he got injured, Mamma. He wanted to ski Bishop's Cauldron. I wouldn't listen and he came after me."

"Don't blame yourself. Spring skiing is dangerous. You shouldn't have gone in the first place."

Bella lifted her head. "But I *did* go. Luca saved my life and told me what to do. He kept *me* alive!" She broke down completely. "I love him so much, you'll never know."

"I've always known how you felt about him," she murmured.

Of course. Her mother knew everything. "How soon can I see him?"

"You can't."

Her unequivocal answer surprised her. "What do you mean?"

"He's been flown to England so a specialist can try to put his leg back together, but that will take another miracle."

"Luca is in England?" she cried in panic. "How long will he be gone?"

"From what I understand it could be a year considering he'll have to undergo physical rehabilitation and all that entails."

The revelation crushed her. "His condition is much worse than what you've told me, isn't it?"

"That's as much as I know."

"Then I'll text him and ask him to phone me when he's able."

"Right now you need to concentrate on your recovery and put the past behind you." Her mother got that steely look on her face.

"What are you saying?"

"It's time you understood what's expected of you, Bella. You are Princess Baldasseri, destined to marry the right prince. You've always known what your future would be. Surely you realize there can be no more Lucas of this world for you."

Bella felt like she'd just been tossed into a void from which there was no return. "You mean—"

"You know exactly what I'm telling you."

Despite weakness, Bella sat up, clutching the sheet. "In other words, you and father are forbidding me to see Luca again."

A strange smile broke out on her mother's face. "Good. I'm glad we finally understand each other. He's not a prince. Now I'll find your father and tell him and the doctor to come in."

Smoldering in pain and rage, Bella stared at her mother's retreating back.

What her parents were doing was *evil*. Barbaric! She wasn't even allowed to get in touch with Luca and confess that the tragedy was all her fault? She needed to ask his forgiveness.

I must help him. I love him.

Where was Vincenzo? She needed to

get a message to Luca through her brother. How soon would he be back to the palace? The doctor and her parents came in the hospital room, but all she could think about was Luca. She fell back against the pillow in agony.

CHAPTER ONE

Bern, Switzerland, ten years later

FOR THE FIRST time in a decade, twenty-six-year-old Princess Bella Baldasseri of Scuol, Switzerland, was finally going to lay eyes on Luca Torriani, the man whose life she'd ruined ten years ago.

Not a day had gone by in all these years that she hadn't suffered over her thoughtlessness. A fleeting moment of throwing caution to the wind to prove her bravery had smashed his dreams forever. Hers too, because she'd never been allowed to talk to him and ask his forgiveness.

After leaving the hospital, she'd tried to reach him on the phone. When she couldn't, she'd sent him letter after letter, begging him to call her so she could ask for his forgiveness. The fact that he never answered one of them proved how much he hated her, and he would have had every right.

She'd pestered her brother to find out what was going on with Luca, but when Vincenzo got back from San Vitano a week later, he had no answer. With his friend in England, they'd had no contact either. Bella believed him implicitly and had to accept the fact that Luca wanted nothing more to do with her.

Perhaps today—the wedding day Vincenzo had planned with his beloved Francesca Visconti—meant that Bella would finally be able to see Luca. He would be standing up for her brother. The two men had been best friends, but after Luca went to England, everything changed. Vincenzo attended college and said they only kept in touch by phone when they could. Today might be her only chance to tell Luca of her deep sorrow.

She thanked God every day and night that Luca *could* stand on both his legs. The surgeon in England must have done spectacular work. But until she could unburden herself to Luca, she'd stay locked in a prison.

Her brother had been living in a prison all his adult life too. Their parents had arranged his engagement to a princess he didn't love. When she broke the engagement, he was free at last to marry the woman *he* chose. But until their mother knew the reason for the break, it took a miracle for Vincenzo's world to change and their mother to give her blessing.

Bella knew Francesca was her brother's whole world, and she couldn't be happier for them. Her soon-to-be sister-in-law had asked her to be a bridesmaid. Bella loved her already. She and her mother, along with Francesca, her mom and Princess Luna, went shopping. After finding the perfect wedding dress, they picked out filmy gowns of pink, purple, lavender and blue chiffon with lace. It had been a lovely day.

Since the death of Bella's father almost a year ago, she'd done what she could to get along with her mother. She'd dated several princes and had even gone along with her parent's idea to spend time with Prince Antoine Beaufort of Orleans, France. Antoine was a very attractive man who'd been pursuing her for the last few months. Four nights ago, they'd met in Geneva for dinner and dancing. He'd taken her out on the terrace overlooking the lake and admitted that he'd fallen in love with her.

"Will you marry me, Bella?"

As she looked into his anxious eyes, she realized how very much she cared for him.

"Oh, Tonio. I didn't expect a proposal this soon, but I know you'll make a wonderful husband. Will you give me time to think about it? My brother's wedding is coming up this next weekend. After that I have a week of charity commitments taking me out of town. When it's over, I'll phone you and we'll meet wherever you'd like so we can really talk about our feelings and everything else."

"I admit I'm disappointed, but I can wait another week. No longer."

The Beaufort family had been friends of her parents for years. Bella knew both mothers wanted the relationship to end in marriage. He deserved her full attention, but until she'd seen Luca again and had said a final goodbye with her heartfelt apology, she couldn't think clearly.

"I hear you, Tonio, and I promise I'll call.

You're everything a woman could want."
She meant those words and she knew he
could be her future husband if she wanted
it to happen.

The next day she left Geneva to fly back
to Scuol. But instead of dwelling on Antonio's proposal, her mind was elsewhere.
Bella had never forgiven her mother and
father for causing the permanent separation between her and Luca. The hole in
her heart had never closed. Worse, the avalanche that had ruined Luca's dreams for
Olympic greatness had also changed Bella's
life. *Irrevocably.*

Today she would seek him out after the
ceremony and bare her soul to him. This
might be her one and only chance to talk to
him and beg his forgiveness. It was something she had to do, even if she knew he
hated her for what she'd done. Then maybe
she could push past her feelings of guilt and
loss in order to say yes to Tonio. The media
had already hinted there might be another
wedding in the future following in the wake
of her brother's.

She hoped that seeing Luca again would
at last allow her to put the past to bed so she

could fall deeply in love with Tonio. Right now Bella needed reassurance that her feelings for Luca had been nothing more than a residual teenaged crush. It couldn't be anything else. The fact that he'd never reached out to her in ten years *had* to mean that the only feelings of attraction and longing had come from her side. She'd been a fool to think otherwise. That kiss they'd shared that day on the mountain had been nothing more than a reaction to a life-or-death crisis.

Bella drove in a limo from the Bellevue Palace Hotel to the cathedral with her mother and grandparents on her father's side ahead of time. She was sorry that her grandparents on her mother's side couldn't be here to see Vincenzo married.

They used to come to Scuol often. Bella loved them very much.

But her grandmother, Princess Caderina Melis Cossu, had been in a tragic car accident four years earlier. It had killed Bella's grandfather, Prince Alfonsu Cossu, and had left Caderina paralyzed from the waist down. She'd become an invalid and was ill. Since his death, their family flew to the palace in Sardinia to see her when they could. It was a shame her *nonna* was missing this event since she adored Vincenzo and Bella, and they adored her.

With the aid of umbrellas, the family avoided most of the summer rain. They hurried inside and sat on a pew near the altar while they waited. In a few minutes Princess Luna, the darling, pregnant wife of Bella and Vincenzo's cousin Prince Rinieri, joined them dressed in pink chiffon.

But Bella had a problem. Sounds of the organ began to permeate the interior. The church had filled and she couldn't sit still. Any second now the rest of the wedding party would assemble and she'd catch her first sight of Luca.

Her heart jumped when the Bishop in ceremonial robes entered from a side door. Following him came four men all looking magnificent. Vincenzo and Rinieri wore the royal navy dress and gold braid of the House of Baldasseri. Francesca's brother, Rolf, and Luca walked in wearing black tuxes with a white rose in the lapel to match Francesca's bouquet. Again Bella thanked God Luca *could* walk. Tears trickled down her cheeks as they stood on one side of the aisle.

Luca, the eighteen-year-old skier she'd loved and dreamed about all these years, had turned into a tall, virile male with a five-o'clock shadow and dark wavy hair. He was so visibly gorgeous he took her breath and she froze at the sight of him.

The Bishop nodded to the women to come forward. Thank goodness Princess Luna had the wits to give Bella a slight nudge, otherwise she would have remained sitting there in a trance.

If Luca saw her get up, he gave no indication. She felt sick to her stomach to realize this moment had come. Her brother had indicated that he liked Tonio and hoped something might come of that relationship. But other than to tell her that Luca wasn't married yet, Vincenzo kept his silence about everything else.

That vital piece of news didn't mean Luca wasn't involved with some beauty. All the girls at school had been crazy about him. From this brief glimpse of the full-grown man, Bella knew he could have his pick. It killed her to think of him with another woman. She had no idea where he lived, what he'd been doing all these years, what he did for a living. Nothing!

At the sound of the wedding march, she watched Francesca walk down the aisle on the arm of her father. To see father and daughter together so happy sent a fresh pain through Bella. What she would have given to have her own father alive, walking her down the aisle toward Luca. But it could never be. Her mother's words of ten years ago had scarred her soul.

You are Princess Baldasseri, destined to marry the right prince.

The Bishop began speaking. "If the couple will clasp hands, please come before me while the others take their seats and we'll begin with a prayer."

Francesca's mother took the flowers from her daughter and the three women sat down again on the bride's side of the aisle. Bella's eyes followed Luca, who sat on the other side. No longer a simple crush of a sixteen-year-old girl, one sight of Luca and he was still the epitome of Bella's womanly dreams. Yet there was no way she could see more of him right now unless she leaned forward. She would have to wait until the reception at the Visconti villa after they all left the cathedral.

The beautiful ceremony touched her heart when she heard Francesca vow to love and honor Vincenzo for as long as they lived. At that moment her brother added the unscripted words, "And after." He truly was in love with the veterinarian commoner. His joy had begun.

But at the sight of Luca, a new kind of turmoil for Bella was just beginning.

As the beaming bride and groom started down the aisle to greet everyone, Luca Torriani followed the Bishop out the side door to the anteroom. From there he could exit the cathedral from a rear door to a taxi and avoid everyone.

After Vincenzo had begged Luca to stand up for him at his wedding, he'd promised to be there for him. But it had been at a huge cost to him personally. One look at Princess Bella Baldasseri gowned in heavenly blue had destroyed every defense he'd erected to shut her out of his consciousness. Ten years of being away from Scuol hadn't helped anything. The beautiful, fun-loving sixteen-year-old teenager had grown up all right.

She'd become a breathtaking, voluptuous woman. Her hair, a swirling mixture of vanilla and café-au-lait, cascaded over her shoulders. Over the years he'd seen her in the news. Vincenzo had mentioned her during several phone conversations having to do with Prince Antonio. More recently there'd been pictures of her with the Prince. The thought of them together twisted his insides.

Bella had a sensual beauty beyond the physical. It eclipsed that of every woman he'd ever met or dated. While colleagues his age were married and having children, he couldn't be further from that situation. For her to have this effect on Luca when she hadn't reached out to him in all these years made him want to escape Bern right now.

He'd thought she would at least have contacted him after the avalanche, but he never saw or heard from her again. Vincenzo had never volunteered any information. It seemed her interest in Luca had been the simple infatuation of a sixteen-year-old after all. That's how little he'd meant to her and Vincenzo's silence on the subject said it all.

The last thing he'd wanted to do was participate in Vincenzo's wedding because it meant seeing her again. But the two men had been like blood brothers in their teenage years. Luca had to put in an appearance at his friend's reception before leaving.

The only thing that helped was Vincenzo's promise he would arrange for Luca to sit at a table with Daniel Zoller and his wife. Luca had always enjoyed the well-known vet. Over the years Vincenzo had visited Daniel at the vet clinic in Zernez many times. First there was his golden retriever, Rex, and then his Bernese mountain dog puppy he'd named Karl. Luca had loved both of Vincenzo's dogs, not being able to have one of his own.

By an amazing stroke of fate, seven years later Francesca Visconti, first known as Dr. Linard, had been hired as a new vet at the Zoller clinic. She'd looked after a dying Karl when Vincenzo had taken him in. Talk about love at first sight for Vincenzo, even though he was engaged to Princess Valentina at the time! He deserved this happiness after years of doing the princely duty he was born to. What a hell of a life it had been for him until now.

When the taxi reached the Visconti villa, Luca noticed a dozen or more photographers from various news outlets and tabloids already covering the Baldasseri wedding. Following the rumors of another Baldasseri marriage about to take place, they were eager to capture photos of Bella with her future prince. The thought gutted him.

Luca told the chauffeur to drive around the side where he slipped out of the taxi. While he waited for Dr. Zoller to arrive in one of the limos, he made some phone calls. Anything to avoid seeing Bella until he had cover.

The guests began to show up. Luca could pretend he was looking for Daniel, but his heart raced out of rhythm while he watched for the one woman who'd dominated his existence since he was ten. He'd never forget the moment he'd met her.

Vincenzo had invited him to the palace after school. They ran out in back to play and found his eight-year-old sister, Bella.

Luca noticed her sitting on the grass with a golden retriever. She was sobbing her heart out.

When she saw them coming, she lifted her pretty blonde head. Her eyes looked like beautiful wet violets. "There's something wrong with Rex's left leg, Vincenzo. I found him lying here. We have to help him! I know *you* can fix him."

"I'll ask Papa to drive us to the vet. Be right back, Bella."

He raced off, leaving the two of them alone.

She stared at him. "Who are you?"

"Luca."

"Do you like dogs?"

"I'd love one of my own, but my mother is allergic to them so we can't have one."

"That's sad. You can come over here any time and play with Rex when he's better."

He'd been touched by her friendliness and that she loved her brother and dog so much. Luca didn't have siblings. The meeting that day was the beginning of a three-way friendship that didn't end until the two of them were caught in the avalanche.

His thoughts had taken him back so far,

he hadn't been watching for Dr. Zoller. By now most of the guests, if not all, would have arrived. That meant Bella was here too. He took a deep breath and walked around to the front of the villa to face a barrage of cameras he ignored. Signora Visconti, Francesca's mother, greeted him at the door.

"Come in, Luca."

"It was a beautiful ceremony, *signora*."

"I agree, and your being here for Vincenzo means everything to him. He told me you'd be sitting with Dr. Zoller and his wife since you know him. Walk through the foyer to the left."

A dozen tables decorated with linen cloths and flowers filled the room. The guests had found their places. Luca made straight for the vet's table situated near the back. He had one friend here. Being with Daniel and his wife helped him to relax.

They'd just started to relive memories of Vincenzo and his dogs when Francesca's father stood up to make a speech. It forced Luca to look in that direction. He dreaded the sight of Bella sitting next to Prince Antonio. Out of the corner of his eye he saw her seated at a table with her cousin Prince

Rinieri and his wife, Princess Luna. For some reason Prince Antonio wasn't with her. He wondered why, but figured the man had other princely duties to attend to.

The three of them radiated a kind of royal splendor that cut through him like a knife. Bella had matured into her princess world and had lost interest in Luca years ago. What an idiot to believe she'd ever yearned to see him again.

Just last evening Vincenzo had indicated that the Prince would be a great catch for his sister. He really liked him. That did it. Right now Luca had to force himself to concentrate on the meal being served.

Before long everyone made toasts, then it came Luca's inevitable turn. He'd come prepared and got to his feet with his champagne glass in hand.

"Dante once wrote that a great flame follows a little spark. Apparently there was more than a little spark the day Vincenzo took his sick dog, Karl, to the vet. One look at the gorgeous Dr. Linard and he was lit by the brightest light in the firmament."

"Francesca is that," Daniel whispered with a smile as Luca sat back down. "The clinic can't do without her. It's going to be a fight between me and Vince for her attention. We know who will win."

Luca nodded. Francesca adored her new husband. Lucky man.

Before long the ecstatic couple was ready to leave. Francesca turned and threw the bouquet behind her. It fell into the hands of... Bella. Intentional or otherwise, that did it for Luca.

With his stomach churning, he left the room and hurried out to the side of the villa to call for a taxi. The rain had turned to drizzle. As soon as he could return to the hotel where he'd stayed the night, he would change his clothes and head for the airport.

Five minutes later he walked around to the front. The taxi turned into the drive at the same time. But before he could climb in the back, he felt a hand on his arm.

"May I ride with you?" sounded a trembling voice he would never forget.

CHAPTER TWO

BELLA HELD HER breath waiting for Luca to answer.

He turned, impaling her with those stunning green eyes that had haunted her dreams for years. "Is it allowed, Princess?" His cold, deep voice permeated to her insides, cutting her to the core.

She shivered, realizing how much he despised her, but she refused to run from him until she'd bared her soul. "After I ruined your life, you have every right to tell me to go to blazes."

His dark brows furrowed. "What are you talking about?"

"You know exactly what I did, Luca, and I've never gotten over it. Please hear me out," she begged. "I—"

"Signorina!" the driver exclaimed, interrupting her. "Are you coming or not?"

"Quick, Bella. We're blocking the other cars. Get in the taxi." Luca helped her with her gown and slid in next to her before closing the door. After telling the driver where to take them, he turned to her. "Start again from the beginning. Explain to me how you ruined my life. Whatever gave you that idea?" He sounded so matter-of-fact, she didn't know what to think.

"You don't have to pretend, Luca. We both know you warned me not to go down Devil's Gulch, but I did it anyway to show off in front of you and prove I wasn't afraid."

"Wait a minute. *That's* what you're talking about? Something that happened so long ago I hardly remember?"

Tears gushed from her eyes. "How can you say that when I think about it every day!" she exploded in pain.

"Why?"

"Because of me you got caught in the avalanche that ended your skiing career. I'll never forgive myself for what I did."

"As I recall, I admired your fearlessness."

"You *couldn't* have. It was a facade anyway." Scalding tears kept running down her face, but she couldn't hold them back and needed to finish this apology. "When we heard the crack and saw what was coming from above, you skied down to help me. It was *my* willfulness that put your life in danger. I understand why you hate me so terribly and never came near."

"Never came near—" he murmured as if deep in thought. She thought he sounded bewildered. "Blame didn't come into it."

She heard the old caring Luca in his voice. Her heart wanted to believe him. "Of course it did. What I did ended your chance to ski in the Olympics. I'm *so* sorry." Bella forgot they weren't teenagers. She sobbed and buried her wet face in her hands, oblivious to everything but her need to ask his forgiveness.

"It was my choice to come after you."

"And look what happened—Mother told me they operated on your right leg all day, hoping to save it, but you would never ski again. You can't imagine the depth of my agony when I heard that. I tried to visit you while we were both in the hospital, but I wasn't allowed."

In the semidarkness, a look of real anger

darkened those green orbs. "Who prevented you from coming to my room?"

Surprised at his fierce change in tone, she wiped her eyes. "Mother. She said—"

"We've arrived!" The driver broke in once again, sounding impatient. She hadn't realized they'd stopped in front of a hotel.

Luca grasped her hand. "Come on, Bella. We need privacy to talk."

She got out the best she could in her long bridesmaid gown, breathing in the warm night air. Everyone outside stared at the two of them while he paid the driver. A few people took pictures with their phones. Still clutching her hand, they walked inside the hotel to the elevator. The guests stopped talking to watch them.

The elevator couldn't enclose them fast enough. Luca's eyes played over her. "Don't be surprised if a picture of us coming into the hotel is on the front page of tomorrow's news. How will you explain this to Prince Antonio? The news has hinted at a marriage between the two of you."

"We're not engaged yet, Luca. The journalists get away with speculation all the time, the way they always do," she bit out.

"Because of Vincenzo's wedding, today's pictures will be splashed all over anyway. I couldn't care less. My life has been a nightmare. What else is new?"

Not engaged yet? Why in heaven's name had Bella's life been a nightmare? It made no sense.

Luca took her to his suite on the third floor and shut the door. "The restroom is down the hall. While you freshen up, I'll get us something to drink. Do you still like cola?" They used to drink it when they went on picnics in the mountains.

She smiled at him. It lit up the dark places in his soul. "Always."

"It's nice to know some things don't change. Two colas coming up. Then we'll talk." He needed answers to questions he'd been waiting for all these years.

"Thank you. I'll be right back."

The fact that she'd never come near him or talked to him since that fateful day pretty well told its own story. He hadn't been on her mind, and it was a fact she *was* involved with a prince Vincenzo approved of. Despite her denials, there wasn't much more to be said. It shocked Luca that he could feel such jealousy at this point.

Impatient with himself, he disappeared into the bedroom and changed into a navy pullover and jeans. After a trip to the kitchenette for drinks, he went in the living room and sat down on the couch to wait for her.

When she came in, she stopped in her tracks. "It's not fair that you've changed into something comfortable."

"You're welcome to put on my robe. It's hanging on the back of the bathroom door." He hadn't meant it to sound provocative.

She flashed him a surprising grin. "I better not. What if there's a house fire and we have to evacuate? Imagine the shocking images spread all over the media."

He laughed. Bella's spirit was like no one else's and she seemed surprisingly unchanged. More like the girl he'd once known and loved. She sat down in one of the upholstered chairs and put her small jeweled purse on the nearby end table. He'd placed her cola there and they both drank a little.

"Where's that fearlessness you displayed years ago?"

"I lost it on the day my actions meant you might not ever walk again. When I saw you enter the cathedral earlier today, I thanked God all over again that you could still stand on your own two legs. Your recovery is an answer to prayer."

Her anguish tore him up. He'd never forget how she'd broken down in the taxi. To be that close to her had been a torment for him. "What exactly did your mother say to prevent you from coming into my hospital room?"

"She said you'd been flown to England where a specialist could work on your leg and try to put it back together. The implication was that you still might lose it."

"Your mother told you *what*?" Luca shot to his feet, incredulous. "That was a lie!"

She stared up at him. "I—I don't understand," her voice faltered. "You weren't flown there?"

"Hell, no. I was right there in the hospital, frantically trying to call you from the pay phone since I'd lost my cell."

"*You* tried to phone me?"

"Of course. I wanted to know how you were. The doctor said you escaped with no broken bones, but I wanted to hear it from you. Unfortunately your phone wasn't working. I almost went out of my mind." When she didn't try to reach him, he'd assumed he wasn't that important to her. When he'd eventually talked to Vincenzo, he'd deflected any inquiries about his sister, until Luca finally got the message. It hurt soul deep.

"That's because I lost my cell in the avalanche too and my parents bought me a new one. I kept trying to phone you, but there was no service. My mind melted down completely," she lamented. "In desperation, I started writing you letters, but you never answered. I must have written sixty of them."

"Sixty—but then what...?"

"Yes. Finally I had to realize you despised me for what I'd done and so I stopped trying to reach you."

Luca stopped pacing because he believed her. "It's all starting to make a ghastly kind of sense."

"What do you mean?"

Over all these years, nothing was as he'd imagined. He turned to her. "Please go on.

I want to hear the rest before I explain this riddle."

"Riddle?"

She really didn't know?

"Maybe *mystery* would be a better word."

Bella stared up at him. "When I asked mother how long you would have to be in England, she said you could be gone a year. She explained you would have to undergo rehabilitation."

"For a whole year?" He was incredulous.

"Yes," her voice quavered. "But when school ended in May and there was still no word from you, I believed you hated me for what I'd done. I couldn't bear it and believed that was why I never heard from you."

Luca bit out an epithet. "I could never hate you, Bella."

"Even so, I—I went into a depression," she stammered. "My parents booked a suite at the Chateau d'Ouchy on Lake Geneva and we vacationed there for a month with their friends. I spent time with Princess Constanza in Lausanne. They hoped the vacation would help, but it didn't."

"So *that's* where you went." His words

sounded more like a hiss. "I saw one of the kitchen boys from the palace in town. He said you'd all gone on vacation, but he didn't know where."

Tears filled her eyes again. "The second we returned to Scuol, I sneaked out of the palace and went straight to the health clinic to see your father in the allergy department. Though I was forbidden to see you again and knew you hated me, I was determined to get answers about you even though I'd never met him."

So Bella *had* tried to see him too! His mind reeled. These revelations changed so many things for him, he was stunned. "What did you find out?" He held his breath.

"It turned out to be a very short trip because…because I learned that your family had *moved* from Scuol! No one in Dr. Torriani's old office knew where he'd gone. He'd left his practice with no forwarding address. It was as if you'd vanished off the face of the earth! I decided you wanted to get away from me after what I'd done."

Luca heard her agony, but didn't dare sweep her in his arms. If he did that, he'd never let her go. "I had no idea."

The sobs kept coming. She clutched at her gown. "After I went home to the palace in devastation, I ran to my parents' bedroom and demanded they tell me the truth. Do you know what Papa said?

"Bella, sweetheart—you must remember what we've told you. You are Princess Baldasseri, destined to marry the right prince. You're an adult now and must accept your fate."

A groan came out of Luca.

"From that moment on I realized my parents were in total charge and I wouldn't be allowed to see you ever again. I began to understand that Vincenzo must have been warned off too. It explained his silence. With Papa's words, it was as if the world I thought I'd known had blown up in my face."

"And mine," Luca whispered, needing desperately to comfort her. "There's no question we were both betrayed, but not by Vincenzo. No better man on earth exists. I have the gut feeling your parents and my father decided to intervene in our lives to get the job done."

"*Your* father—"

He nodded. "It took teamwork and had to be him. You never knew him. He's a good man who did everything for me. But if he'd been born royal, he would have invented the divine right of kings."

A half smile broke the corner of her delectable mouth. "I heard a lot of emotion behind that statement. Tell me."

"My *papa* married late and dominated my sweet mother, who couldn't have more children after I was born. His father was a doctor too. They made a good living. Papa was determined to support me to the best advantage—the best schools, the best education, the best friends.

"Everything went along fine until I met Vincenzo. Papa had an innate revulsion toward royalty and was furious that you and your brother were attending public school. He didn't consider royals to be a useful part of society."

"Your father had a point, Luca."

"Papa wouldn't believe it if he heard you say that."

"Not all of us are prigs."

Deep laughter came out of him. "The last thing he wanted was for me to have anything to do with your brother. But he couldn't stop me from being friends with him at school.

"One day I brought your brother to the house on his eleventh birthday. My father took one look at him and turned into someone I didn't know. It hurt me that he left the room without saying anything to him."

"How awful."

"It was. Mamma baked a cake for him as a favor to me. The three of us had a little party. She told me later that he didn't act like a prince and she loved him. In fact, she said that if she could have more children, she'd like one just like Vincenzo."

More tears came to Bella's eyes. "I love your mother without meeting her, Luca. She sounds wonderful."

"She is, and she would love you because you're like Vincenzo in many ways. But because of my father, you'll understand why I always played at the palace. Meeting you made it even more fun. I had the happiest childhood memories there that anyone could have had."

Bella sucked in her breath. "So did I. But it all ended on that horrible day." She looked into his eyes. "Tell me everything from the moment you got home from the hospital."

He checked his watch. Luca didn't know where to start and now wasn't the moment. "That'll take some time and I have a plane to catch. I should already have left for the airport. Vincenzo told me you're staying with the Visconti family so I need to take you back there on the way."

"Can't you stay until tomorrow?"

"I wish I could, but I have to be back for work in the morning."

"You work on a Sunday?"

"Sometimes. Tomorrow is one of those days. Why don't you finish your drink while I grab my suitcase. Then we'll go."

Bella walked over to the end table for her cola. She should be grateful to have had this much time to apologize to him. Her prayers had been answered. But the teenage Bella would have begged him to take her with him.

Except that you're not sixteen anymore, and Luca has been playing by the rules for the last ten years.

He'd stopped thinking about her a long time ago. She imagined he was involved with a gorgeous woman right now and anxious to get back to her. The lucky man didn't have photographers following his every step.

They took a taxi for the short trip back to the Visconti villa.

She couldn't stand it that he was leaving, but his reasons were none of her business. "Luca? Before you go, I have to know about your leg. How bad was it? I want the truth."

"It did require some surgery but my surgeon was a genius and I recovered quickly. I can still ski if I want to, just not competition."

"Honestly?" she cried for joy. "You have no idea how happy that makes me. If you'd had the opportunity, I know you would have become an Olympian."

"It would have been exciting for a while, yet it was more my father's dream than mine."

"You're his only son."

"Just as you are your mother's only daughter. We both know her dream for you. Maybe you're not engaged to Prince Antonio yet, but I imagine it will happen any time soon. Vincenzo says he's a good man. That means a lot. And I noticed Francesca's bridal bouquet was tossed at you."

Trying to convince Luca of anything was like talking to a rock wall. "That was bad aim on her part since it was meant for Gina, not me." They reached the villa way too soon and she was frantic. "There are still so many questions I want to ask you, but I know I should be grateful you've given me this much of your time."

"I'm sorry I have to rush away, Bella."

"Please don't apologize."

After the driver pulled to a stop, Luca told him to wait while he helped Bella get out. They walked to the entrance. She wanted to fling herself in his arms and never let him go.

To her surprise, he suddenly reached in his wallet and pulled out a business card he handed to her. "Perhaps this will answer some of those questions. *Adia*, Bella," he said in Romansh. *"Buna fortuna."*

Good luck in the future?

Clearly he didn't expect them to meet again. He'd moved on with his life.

Dying inside, she watched him stride on those long powerful legs to the taxi and get in. After it drove away taking her heart, she rang the bell. Rolf, Francesca's brother, opened the door with his usual smile.

"Bella—come on in. Gina and I wondered where you disappeared to."

"I spent a little time with Luca. He just brought me back on his way to the airport. Where's Gina?"

"In the study. My parents have gone to bed."

"That sounds good to me too. You go back to Gina. I'm going upstairs to change out of this gown."

Once in her room, she sat down on the side of the bed to look at the card clutched in her hand.

Luca Torriani, MD
Sports Medicine
Julier Medical Clinic
Suite 6
Saint Moritz, Switzerland

It gave the clinic's business number. All this time Luca had only been an hour away, and he'd become a doctor, *just like his father.* She felt like she'd been stabbed all over again.

After these many years of wondering, the card did answer where Luca lived and worked, but she knew nothing about his personal life. She spent the rest of the night in utter turmoil.

The chauffeur drove Luca to the Bern Belp Airport. It had done wonders for him that Bella had appeared upset because he'd been forced to leave. Those violet eyes of hers had pled with him to stay. The drive away from her constituted a fresh new agony.

During his flight back to Saint Moritz, Switzerland, he went over every detail of their conversation in his mind. Luca now understood the cruel thing their families had done to keep them apart. When he'd never heard from Bella again, he'd been forced to accept what had happened. He was a commoner and could never be Bella's choice. She'd been forced to accept the situation too. Since the avalanche, they hadn't seen or talked to each other. *Not until tonight.*

It tugged at him that she'd wanted to

keep talking, but he'd had to pull away to catch this flight. The pain in her eyes had prompted him to give her his business card. What she did or didn't do with it was up to her.

He drove back to his apartment and checked his messages before going to bed. But getting any sleep was futile while he tried to fit the missing pieces of a ten-year puzzle together. They all led back to their parents' subterfuge. By morning he'd reached the boiling point.

After getting through his hospital rounds, he received a text from his mother. His parents expected him for Sunday dinner that evening. He knew what his father wanted. Luca was sick to death of his watchdog tactics. The bullying and rage may have subsided to some degree, but his father was like a hunting dog, always on point.

His parent had been furious that Luca had agreed to be part of Vincenzo's wedding party. It didn't take a genius to realize what was really going on in the older man's mind. His fears of Luca and Bella getting together had dominated his father's life ever since Luca had met Vincenzo in grade school. Luca decided to drive over to their house now and have it out with them.

"Mamma?" he called out after letting himself in.

"Ah, Luca—you're back from Bern!" She came running into the living room from the kitchen to hug him. "This is much better than a text. Come in the kitchen and I'll fix you some lunch."

"I'd rather stay right here." He drew her to the couch. "Where's Papa?"

"He ran to the store for some pipe tobacco after I got home from church. He'll be back soon. How was the wedding?"

"Incredible, but right now the three of us need to talk about what happened ten years ago."

Her smile faded and a haunted look crossed over her face, but she said nothing.

"After the wedding, I spent time with Bella. We pieced everything together. I now know that our two families purposely kept us apart all these years."

Tears filled her eyes. "Luca—" She pressed his arm. "I didn't know anything about what your father and Bella's mother did until Vincenzo came to see me a few years after you left for the States. He loves you and felt it wrong that I never knew. I loved him for telling me the truth, but by then the damage had been done to you and Bella. I didn't want to dredge it all up for you then, not after so much time had passed."

Luca hugged her against him. "I couldn't believe you had any part in it."

"What the two of them did went against God. Your father did a terrible thing by tearing up the letters Bella wrote to you. He told Bella's mother triumphantly—that's how Vincenzo found out about it. I am so ashamed of his actions. He never learned about Vincenzo's visit, but I've been in pain ever since. You know I love you heart and soul and have only wanted your happiness."

"Grazie Dio." He rocked her in his arms. His father had torn up Bella's heart and Luca's. "You have to know how much I love you. Thank you for telling me about the letters and Vincenzo, but you need to understand I'm not letting Papa or Bella's mother rule my life ever again."

"That's good, *figlio mio.* It's wonderful that you and Bella have reconnected. Live your life the way God intended—the way *I* always wanted you to live it." She kissed his cheek.

"That I plan to do. Forgive me if I don't come for dinner. I have other plans for today. I'll call you tomorrow." After another hug, he left the house and drove to his apartment to change clothes. The thought of being inside four walls would be unbearable.

CHAPTER THREE

THE BRIGHT SUN practically blinded Luca as he headed for the mountains. He reached for his sunglasses and took off. As he turned onto the main road, his phone rang. No doubt his father wanted to know why he wasn't coming for dinner and would insist Luca drop by at some point.

Luca had anticipated this latest response and let his phone ring.

Though seeing Bella again had turned Luca inside out, the truth remained that she'd moved on. For that reason, his father's worries made no sense, yet the ringing didn't stop. He reached for the phone to decline the call. But he caught himself in time when he saw the caller ID. It was the clinic's answering service. He clicked on. "This is Dr. Torriani."

"I have a patient needing to talk to you.

She said it's an emergency, yet hung up before leaving her name. Here's the number."

He made a note and phoned it. One of his patients had to be in trouble.

"Luca?" a familiar voice sounded.

His heart leaped into his throat. "Bella?" Handing her his card had been an experiment of sorts. He hadn't expected a response this fast.

"Yes! I'm so glad you answered. I'm in Saint Moritz at the train station."

She was here? He shook his head in disbelief. "Say that again."

"I know this is a surprise. I flew to Chur early this morning, then took the Bernina Express, knowing it would pass through Saint Moritz. It'll be leaving to go on to Pontresina in about fifteen minutes. I wondered if you have enough time to take the train with me that far so we can talk. We didn't have enough time last night. Would it be possible, or do you have other plans?"

Luca was so blown away to hear from her, he didn't stop to consider anything else. "I will leave for the station now."

"That's wonderful!" she cried. "When you walk through the train car, you'll see me wearing a slouchy black winter hat and sunglasses." All that glorious blond hair covered up made sense. Otherwise, the photojournalists would notice her immediately. She thought of everything!

"I'll be in a sage-colored crew neck sweater."

"I'd know you anywhere."

Bella. "See you soon." He clicked off, stunned that she was in Saint Moritz, that she'd dared to reach out to him knowing what could happen. He'd thought she'd be traveling back to the palace with her family once they left Bern.

After he'd parked at the station, he went inside and bought a first-class round-trip ticket. He had no idea where to find her as he hurried out to the platform. The only thing to do was climb on board and walk from car to car.

In the next-to-the-last car, he spotted her. No matter how she'd disguised herself, Bella was an absolute knockout and every male eye noticed her. She wore black pants and a fitted short-sleeved black top with gold buttons that hugged her waist. If she saw him, she gave no indication. He knew her bodyguard from the palace followed her everywhere, day or night.

The car was full except for one vacant seat opposite her on the side of the aisle. Somehow, she'd arranged it. He sat down and the train took off for Pontresina. Outside the window he saw the passing landscape of the Engadin.

She sat forward. "I'm so thrilled you answered your phone and could come with me. It was a chance in a million."

"It worked." He smiled at her breathlessness. "You know, of course, your mother will be told what you're doing."

"That doesn't matter. Why don't we sit back and enjoy the scenery out of these gigantic windows? A trolley is coming by if you want a drink."

"I'm not thirsty yet. I thought you'd still be with your family."

"After being with you such a short time last night, Luca, I needed more time to talk with you. I had to hope that your business card meant you might want to talk too. But if this causes complications for you because of a woman you're involved with, I totally understand."

Luca had never known anyone more honest. He sucked in his breath, ignoring her comment about another woman. "I did hope we could talk again down the road."

"But you didn't expect me to take it several forbidden steps further. Today is a case in point, and now that I've come, you don't know what to do with me."

Her frankness took his breath. If only she knew what was going on inside of him. "How did you happen to fly to Chur?"

"It's a long story. I'll tell you everything later. Here comes the trolley. I'll grab a cola."

Out of the corner of Luca's eye, he watched her drink. Everything she said and did had always fascinated him. Nothing had changed for him where she was concerned. Ten years had turned her from the girl he'd loved into the woman he desired beyond all else.

"Let's hear your long story."

She still wore her sunglasses, but he knew she was staring at him. "I wanted to see you again, so I convinced the family that I had important work to do and took a roundabout way of meeting you."

What important work?

"It was a risk to myself, of course, but by some miracle you were available. I don't think my bodyguard has figured it out quite yet. He's assuming I have business in Pontresina as well as Chur. What's nice is that I have friends there I've done business with before."

That sounded like the adventurous and creative Bella he'd always been crazy about. "So what's the plan?"

"When we reach Pontresina, I'm taking a taxi to Oberengadin Hospital, where I've met people in the past. You come in the front entrance after I've been inside a few minutes. There's a drinking fountain around the corner to the left on the ground floor. I'll send someone to show you where I'll be."

She recrossed her long legs, drawing his attention to the fabulous way she looked. "I think it's time to change the subject to something happy. What were you going to do today?"

"Go for a hike."

"That sounds like heaven."

"I'm perfectly content to be here with you, Bella."

"I feel the same way. We'll be getting off any second now."

Luca had been in Pontresina before, hiking with friends. As they arrived in the alpine village surrounded by pine trees giving off a pungent scent, the train slowed to a stop.

Bella got up. "See you in a few minutes."

Luca couldn't take his eyes off her womanly figure. He waited until she'd disappeared from sight before leaving the car himself. After looking around outside, there was no sign of Bella. Most likely her bodyguard had already followed her to the hospital. Luca found a taxi that drove him there.

A smile broke out on his face. Even though he knew she was being watched, this cloak-and-dagger stuff had started to appeal to him. Luca hadn't had this much fun in ages. When his father heard about it, he'd erupt, but Luca was impervious to him. He walked inside and found the drinking fountain around the corner.

"Dr. Torriani?" He turned to the thirty-ish female wearing a white hospital coat. "If you'll follow this hallway to the end and turn to the left, there's an examination room on your right where your party is waiting."

"Thank you."

When he reached the said room, he knocked on the door and Bella let him inside. He shut the door and they sat down. "You know we're not fooling anyone, don't you, Princess? Word will get back to Prince Antonio that you've been with me twice since the wedding. Isn't that living a little dangerously, even for you?"

The moment the words came out, she stiffened and he knew he'd offended her.

"Maybe, but it gives security something to do. I'll face the consequences later."

"How will you get to Scuol?"

Her softly rounded chin lifted. "In my royal helicopter waiting here in back for me."

He grimaced. "I've upset you. You know I didn't mean to and I apologize."

She stared at him, but he could see her lower lip trembling and wanted to kiss it quiet.

"You can't help it can you, Luca. You haven't forgiven me, and my title is so ingrained in you, I'm lit up in neon lights where you're concerned. Unfortunately, this foolish escapade of mine will cause you more distress once your father hears about it, and he will."

"Bella—" he said on a groan. "Forget my father and listen to me. I could have refused to meet you at the station and that would have been the end of it. After seeing each other last night, we both know we need to talk again."

"Really? Or are you just here because you and Vincenzo are blood brothers? You don't want to upset me because you know it will upset him."

His jaw tautened. "This isn't about Vincenzo."

"I hardly think it's about me, his little sister. You're too saintly for that."

He cringed. "Saintly? Be honest. You and I have always had a special connection."

"Maybe *gentlemanly* would be the better word. You see me as a 'special' friend. I threw myself at you in high school and you handled it with mastery. How you must have dreaded Vincenzo's wedding! You knew I'd be there. Only your love for my brother would have caused you to put up with me again. I'm the woman who ruined your chances for Olympic fame, let alone damaged your leg forever. You'll never get over it."

He couldn't believe they were having this conversation again. "I thought we'd resolved all that." He shook his head. "You have a picture of our situation that's completely wrong." Her lack of interest in him after the avalanche had kept him away from her, nothing else.

"I don't think so," she came back. "Your father was right to move your family to Saint Moritz without telling a single soul. He knew what he was doing so the princess couldn't find you. *I* am that said princess, my most hated word in any language. From the moment I was conceived, it became a birthright I haven't been able to escape."

"Stop, Bella—" he blurted in frustration.

"I *can't* stop. Hear me out, Luca. You were born a Torriani, with the title of doctor, son of a doctor. Our two paths were never meant to cross, let alone converge. Forgive me for having phoned you. It was a mistake."

"Why would I have to forgive you for

anything when *I* was the one who gave you *my* card?"

"It doesn't matter."

"But it does, and I have something vital to tell you." In fact the matter of the destroyed letters would crucify her.

She shook her head. "It's too late. Goodbye, Luca."

Bella jumped up to leave, but Luca grabbed her and pulled her close. "If you won't listen to words, maybe you'll understand this." He lowered his head and his mouth closed over hers in a long passionate kiss. He'd dreamed of this moment for so long, he refused to let her go. She eventually pulled out of his arms, leaving both of them breathless. "Think about that while you're in flight, Bella."

She flew out of the room. Luca could have run after her, but there were people in the hall. This hospital was no place for the no-holds-barred conversation he needed to have with her. Bella's white-hot pain had been building since the avalanche. He understood it because his pain had also reached its zenith.

He heard the helicopter lift off. When

it was out of ear sound, he took the short train trip back to Saint Moritz. It gave him time to plan his next move. She needed to know what his mother had verified about the letters, including Vincenzo's visit with the truth. Now would be a good time to send her a text.

The helicopter flew Bella back to the palace that evening. Luca's unexpected, consuming kiss had turned her world inside out. She trembled the whole way home, trying to understand where it had come from.

As she hurried into the palace and raced up the stairs, her mother called to her. No... Not now. But she had to kiss her and the grandparents good-night. As soon as she could, she hurried to her suite to get ready for bed.

Before climbing under the covers, she reached for her phone. Her heart almost jumped out of her chest when she saw a text from Luca.

When she'd left his arms and had run outside the hospital to the helicopter, she hadn't known what to expect. With hands shaking, she clicked on his text.

Bella. I believe you meant it when you said goodbye to me today. I also meant it when I said you have a picture of our situation that's completely wrong. Of course I think of you as a special friend, but there's a lot more to it than that. That kiss should have told you something! If you ever *want* to know more, you know where to find me.

Bella read and reread it. Did she truly have a faulty picture of their relationship? His kiss had felt so real, she knew she'd never get to sleep and decided to call her *nonna* in Sardinia. It wasn't too late.

"I'm so happy you've phoned me, *bimba*." That was the Italian endearment she'd always used with Bella. "I want to hear about the wedding," she said between deep coughs Bella didn't like.

They talked for a while, but her grandmother Caderina's voice sounded trembly and feeble. Maybe she shouldn't have called her. "I wish you could have been there and I miss you, Nonna. How are you? You don't sound well."

"I'm all right. Don't worry about me." More coughing ensued. "What's going on to cause the deep pain I hear in your voice? Problems with Prince Antonio?"

"No. Nothing like that. After Vincenzo's wedding reception at the Visconti villa, I met with Luca last night, and again today in Saint Moritz."

"Ah."

Yes, ah. "It's been ten years and—" But that was all Bella managed to get out before she broke down sobbing. "Oh, Nonna—I've made such a fool of myself I want to die.

"We had enough time to figure out my parents and his father purposely kept us apart for the last ten years. But as for everything else, my head is a mess. Mother wants me to marry Antonio. He's a wonderful man, but I can't say yes to his proposal yet. Not when I feel the way I do over Luca." Her whole face glistened with moisture.

"And how *do* you feel?"

"The truth is, if I can't be with him, I'll never be happy again."

"Does Luca feel the same about you?"

"I don't know. He kissed me, really kissed for the first time this afternoon. Now I'm in agony."

"Why?"

"Because I don't know if it meant to him what it meant to me. I engineered both meetings. Luca thinks I'm marrying Tonio. I'm so confused I could die."

"But remember, *bimba*—" Bella had to wait for another coughing spasm from her grandmother to subside. "He was willing to risk seeing you twice since the ceremony. Doesn't that tell you anything?"

"Yes, that he doesn't want to offend me. I would give anything on earth if I hadn't been born a princess. You probably think I'm horrible to say that."

"Of course I don't. If you dislike it that much, then do something about it."

Bella swallowed hard. "You wouldn't hate me for it?"

Her grandmother laughed and coughed. "I love you no matter what. You're in charge of your own life, *bimba*. As for Luca, if his kiss made your dreams come true, he meant it. I liked him very much during the times I met him at the palace with your brother. He has a strength about him I admire. Why don't you put him to the ultimate test and see what happens?"

Bella sat up in the bed. "What kind?"

"That's for you to figure out." There was too much coughing now. "You're a clever girl and will find a way." At this point her grandmother could hardly speak.

"Nonna? We've talked too long and you're ill. I'll call you again soon. Right now you need to rest your voice. I love you more than you know. God keep you."

Worried about her grandmother's health, she clicked off before getting under the covers. But in the back of her mind, her *nonna's* admonitions kept taunting her. *Put Luca to the ultimate test.* What kind? What did she mean?

For the rest of the night she tossed and turned reliving their kiss, and trying to figure out what Luca had really meant. At five in the morning, she got out of bed and wrote a special email to her great uncle King Leonardo. Her *nonna* had given her the courage.

As for Luca, she would seek him out again, but this time new tactics were called for. Her grandmother had challenged her to put Luca to the ultimate test. That was exactly when she intended to do.

* * *

On Friday of that week, Luca had just finished up with his last patient and was dreading the empty weekend when there was a knock on the door. "Dr. Torriani?"

He recognized the voice of the receptionist who'd been hired four months ago. Luca had lost count of the times she'd come back to his office when she knew he was alone. It couldn't go on. He felt minus zero attraction. "*Si*, Adele?"

"I can come again if you're still busy."

"I'm afraid I am. Next time, just buzz me if there's an emergency."

"I don't know if there is one or not." He blinked. "A woman came into the office just now. She doesn't have an appointment and didn't give her name. Dr. Glatz upstairs is still in the building and would be willing to see her, but this woman was insistent it had to be the sports medicine doctor."

Could it possibly be Bella? His heart raced. "I'll come."

Luca got up from his desk and walked out of his office to reception. The second his eyes fastened on Bella standing there, his heart rocked him like a sledgehammer.

After that fiery kiss, it had only taken her five days to respond to his text in person. He could breathe again, but for her sake he needed to keep up the pretense of knowing nothing in front of the receptionist.

She had pulled her glorious dark blond hair back and tied it at the nape with a brown-and-white-print scarf. The style revealed her oval face and high cheekbones. With eyes the color of the sweet violets that grew above the palace in Scuol, she was beauty personified.

Her scarf matched the white blouse with its elbow-length sleeves and chocolate brown linen pants. Brown leather sandals adorned her feet. At five foot seven, Bella was a picture of casual elegance only she could carry off. He feared he might need Dr. Glatz in cardiology.

"I remember seeing you at the wedding," he exclaimed in front of Adele, who stared with a mutinous expression at the two of them.

Bella flashed an illuminating smile. "We were never introduced. I'm Alectrona Cossu." *What?* The sun goddess in Greek mythology? He'd seen paintings of her. Bella looked a lot like her with her long blond hair, and was a hundred times more breathtaking. "Rolf told me you worked here, but I couldn't recall your name."

Pay attention, Luca. "Dr. Torriani."

"From the prominent nobles of the Torriani family in Piedmont?"

"Not the same patriarchal line."

"That explains why you're not an architect or sculptor. But I'm thrilled you're the renowned doctor Rolf told me about."

"He's paid to say that."

Her familiar chuckle delighted him. "I happened to be in this area on business and know a child who's in dire need of your particular skills." The reference to business intrigued him. "Will you forgive me for intruding on your work long enough to make an appointment?"

Luca spread his arms. "As you can see, there are no more patients. Come in my office and we'll talk about it."

He glanced at the receptionist. *"Buon weekend, Adele."*

"E tu, Dottore," she said through gritted teeth.

They walked down the hall to his office.

Once inside, he shut the door hardly able to believe she'd come. "Finally we have the time and space to talk about the things we didn't have time for last weekend, Bella."

She walked around studying his diplomas on the wall while he studied her tantalizing figure. "Columbus, Ohio. You spent all those years in the States studying medicine. You were so far away," her voice trembled. He felt it to his bones.

"Not all. If you'll notice the document behind my desk, I ended up in Freiburg, Germany, to do my residency."

She turned to him. "How long have you practiced here?"

"A year and a half."

She gave him a searching gaze. "What brought you to Saint Moritz?"

"You mean *who*. As soon as I was ready to go into practice, my father suggested I join a medical group here looking for a sports medicine doctor."

He heard her mind working. "Don't tell me. Your parents moved to Saint Moritz ten years ago."

Luca nodded. "He and Mamma bought a home with an office where he sees patients.

But enough about me. Why don't you sit down and tell me what you've been doing all these years while I've been away from my favorite place on earth."

She subsided into a chair near his desk. "You mean our own Garden of Eden?"

Their eyes fused. "Where else?"

"It's still my favorite place too, Luca."

The two of them loved to hike to a special grassy spot above the palace beneath arching tree branches full of leaves. Walking underneath made them feel like they'd entered a cathedral. There'd been something magical, even spiritual about it where they'd seen red deer wander through.

His brows arched. "Have you gone there often?"

She gazed at him through half-veiled lids. "Not since the last time you and I saw two adorable mountain hares living there."

Cherished memories made this conversation hurt too much. He perched on a corner of his desk. "What's the latest news from the palace?"

"Well, the honeymooners are in paradise, and Vincenzo's former intended is going to marry the palace guard with whom she fell in love."

"Sometimes good things do happen to the right people."

She nodded. "*Sometimes* being the operative word."

Bella, Bella. "Getting back to you, I want to catch up. I take it you finished high school. So, what did you do next?"

"Princess Constanza and I grew closer. Our parents had fits when we told them we wanted to attend college in Geneva to learn marketing management. They said a princess didn't do that kind of work. We told them we were living in the modern age and needed some skills in case the revolution came."

Luca burst into laughter. "I can hear you saying it. Only you would think of it. Did you prevail?"

"Yes, but we couldn't neglect our princess duties or avoid meeting suitable future husbands."

His lungs froze. "Prince Antonio for example."

"Yes. Among others."

Of course. Bella's comment did nothing

to help his troubled state of mind. "Tell me what you did after graduation."

"We went to work for a regional manufacturing company."

Incredibile. "You're a wonder, Bella. I'm totally impressed. Are you still working there?"

"No. After a while we both turned in our resignations. She wanted to work in her family's robotic business. I planned to work for my family's timber company. I talked it over with Vincenzo and learned we Swiss don't really export wood, so there was no market for me to build or expand the business outside the country. By then my parents insisted I head some charities and put my new skills to work organizing fundraising events."

She'd aroused his curiosity. "You mentioned you were here on business. Last weekend you indicated the same thing."

"*Princess* business, but I didn't want to draw attention in front of your fascinated receptionist."

"Your instincts were right on. Several days a week my father drops in to see me on my lunch hour and has developed a friendship with Adele. His motives are embarrassingly transparent."

Bella's eyes flashed purple. "I can see why. She's a lovely brunette who couldn't take her eyes off you. It wouldn't surprise me if he's hoping to get the two of you together."

"It'll never happen."

"Because someone else has captured your heart?"

His pulse raced. "Could be."

An impish smile broke the corner of her luscious mouth. "All your father needs to hear is that I paid you a visit today."

His father would find out before long. He had the instincts of a bloodhound. Luca got to his feet. "That reminds me. How did you come to be Alectrona Cossu?"

"I'm amazed Vincenzo never let it slip."

"What do you mean?"

"I was named Princess Bella Alectrona Cossu Baldasseri. My grandmother on my mother's side is a princess from the House of Cossu on Sardinia."

"I know," Luca murmured. "Vincenzo and I talked to her on several occasions when she visited with your family. She had a warmth that made it fun to be with her."

"Now you know why I love her so much. She's been an invalid and isn't expected to live much longer. I talked to her last week and she has a horrible cough that means she could be verging on pneumonia."

"I'm sorry to hear that."

"It really frightened me."

He heard the concern in her voice. "Maybe you need to fly there and see her."

"I plan to."

He cocked his head. "You still haven't explained about Alectrona."

"My mother wanted me to have the name Alectrona because she loves Greek mythology. My father wanted to call me Bella."

"I don't know why *you* couldn't have told me all that years ago."

"Because it's too many names and ghastly. I'd rather be Bella, plain and simple. You should hear Constanza's royal name. It's longer and worse than mine."

Bella had always made him laugh. Every time he was with her, he felt a renewal of life. "When did you get here?"

"I flew in on the helicopter this afternoon. The family thinks I flew to Lausanne to see Constanza. Once I checked into a hotel, I took a taxi here not knowing if you'd be available."

Maybe he was dreaming, "How long can you stay?"

"I have to fly back to the palace tomorrow morning. I'm helping Mamma with my grandfather's eighty-eighth birthday party."

The weekend he'd been dreading was back on again. Luca only had tonight to be with her and explain certain facts. He removed his white coat and hung it in the closet. "We haven't begun to talk. Are you hungry?"

"I am now."

"I'll drive us to a place outside town. They serve skewered beef, *pizzocheri* and truffle fondue to die for. We'll leave by the rear entrance. My car is parked in the private lot in back."

CHAPTER FOUR

BELLA HAD TAKEN up Luca's offer to contact him. Now she intended to find out what had been behind that kiss.

She followed him out to his car, an older-model blue Alpha Romeo sedan. "I remember you and Vincenzo always loved talking about Italian cars like this one. You've remained loyal."

"It's been a reliable car." He helped her in the passenger side. Once she'd buckled up, he drove them out of the alpine resort town of five thousand to a tiny village higher up in the mountains.

Saint Moritz had always been known as a winter paradise, but September had to be the perfect time of year to enjoy the fall before snow started to appear. Being alone with Luca like this was so exciting, she felt feverish.

They wound around a more isolated area and pulled up to a small off-road restaurant that looked more like a cottage. Half a dozen cars were clustered around. He parked the car.

"This is a surprise, Luca. You would never know it's here."

"Alf's is Saint Moritz's best-kept secret. Most tourists don't know about it. That's why I like it."

Her gaze swerved to his. "How did you find it?"

"I've had a patient whose parents own it. When I can't stand my own cooking, I eat at the hospital cafeteria, drop in at the folks or come here."

"Where do you live?"

"In an apartment near my office."

Bella would give anything to see it, but he would have to ask her. They both got out of the car and walked to the entrance. She ached for him to take her arm, anything— but he was careful not to touch her. All she could think about now was Luca's mouth on hers with nothing to prompt it except years of suppressed desire on her part. And his? She needed to find out.

"Luca? *Bainvegni! Co voi?*" A welcoming male voice spoke Romansh as they walked inside. Bella watched a bearded, middle-aged man wearing an apron hurry over and hug Luca hard. A pair of warm blue eyes stared at Bella. "Aren't you Pri—"

"A business associate," Luca cut in. "Alf Engen, meet Signorina Cossu. She's here on important business. Is your truffle fondue on tonight's menu?"

"Always for you, along with Barolo wine. Come with me."

The diners ate in booths shaped like horse-drawn sleighs. Bella smiled at Luca. "This place is as charming as the owner. No wonder you like to come here. He cares for you very much. Tell me about your patient."

"Alf Jr. is a star hockey player. Last year he incurred an AC shoulder injury and the doctor wanted to operate. I was consulted and worked with him. No operation was needed and now he's ready to play this season."

"You worked your magic."

"Dr. Torriani!" another male voice broke in on them. She turned her head to see an attractive dark blond guy in his twenties headed for their booth with their wine and fondue. "Papa said you were here with a blonde goddess. For once he wasn't exaggerating."

His eyes, a sea blue like his father's, studied her with embarrassing male interest before serving them. "I understand you're here on business. How long are you going to be in Saint Moritz? I'm free every night."

Luca actually frowned. "Slow down, Alf. I'm afraid Signorina Cossu has other calls on her time."

"I don't doubt it, but since I have an in with you, how about cutting me a break. What are you doing tomorrow, *signorina*?"

"Tomorrow she'll be busy." Luca's quick, less-friendly answer sent darts of delight through her body.

Alf grinned. "As long as it's not with you, Doc, I can handle it until she's free." His gaze swerved to hers once more. "Where are you staying?"

"With her associates," came the pointed answer.

"Okay, Doc. I was only asking. *Guten appetit.*" He winked at Bella.

When he'd disappeared, she looked at Luca. "He's a handful."

Luca swallowed his wine. "Does this happen with every male you meet?"

She took a sip of hers. He sounded jealous. "I was going to ask you a similar question. In case you didn't know, I planned my visit to your office hoping you'd still be there, and alone. Does every good-looking female staff member stick around after hours, praying you'll take them home?"

"Praying? Your choice of words breaks me up, Bella. Why don't we change the subject? If you were able to stay in Saint Moritz tomorrow, I'd ask you to take a hike with me. I thought we'd follow the Fuorcla Surlej trail. You'd love all the meadows and wildflowers. Further up you'd see the Tschierva glacier."

"Stop!" she cried with a smile. "You're torturing me." It *was* torture to hear his plans for them if she could stay. She ate the last of her food and finished her wine. "Please tell the owners that's the best fondue I've ever eaten."

"I'm glad you enjoyed it." He put some money on the table. "Let's go while it's still busy around here. Otherwise, I won't be able to get rid of you-know-who so easily."

Bella noticed that since Luca's former patient hadn't returned, it appeared he'd gotten the message. You didn't mess with Luca.

Relieved to be back in the car, Luca drove them into Saint Moritz, the playground of athletes and the affluent including royals like Bella's family. Night had fallen. He chose an isolated spot along the shore of Lake Saint Moritz.

"I brought you here because we can't go to my apartment or your hotel room. The pictures of you with me would be plastered all over the news tomorrow. I don't want to be the man to upset the royal family."

"And your father."

"He doesn't run my life any longer. That's all over. I had a private talk with my mother last Sunday. She had no idea what my father and your mother did until Vincenzo told her."

"*My* brother?"

"Yes. While I was in Ohio, he went to her out of love for all of us. I knew deep down she wasn't responsible. She admitted she's been very unhappy with my father ever since." He had yet to tell Bella about the letters his father had torn up. Luca didn't have the heart to tell her that yet.

"Oh, Luca. The poor thing."

"It's a great relief to know the truth. That's why a day in the mountains would have been the prescription for what ails us."

"Except we don't have a disease that can be fixed that way," she reasoned. "We were cruelly torn apart by forces beyond our control at the time so we couldn't even say goodbye. But that doesn't have to be the case now, does it?"

His heart thudded. "What's on your mind?"

"We're both over twenty-one and in charge of our own lives. We're free to live the way we want. Do you think you could get away from your work next weekend? At least for one night?"

"You mean like old times," he murmured.

"Not exactly like that since Vincenzo won't be with us. I always wanted to camp out alone with you." Something was going on with Bella he didn't understand, but he was excited about it. "We'll eat the fish we catch, study the constellations with your telescope and visit our own Garden of Eden to see if the mountain hares are still living there."

Good heavens… This woman had turned into temptation itself, heedless of the consequences to her. He had no magic power to erase her from his consciousness and didn't want to. Over those early years Bella had become part of his DNA.

He turned to her. "I'll come to Scuol next Saturday and go home Sunday." It was only a fifty-five-mile drive. "If you can find a way to meet me at the Garage Lishana on La Via de la Staziun at nine a.m., we'll leave for the mountains from there."

"Isn't that where you had a part-time job?"

"You know it is. For a couple of years, yes. I'll bring all the gear we'll need."

Her eyes glowed purple fire. "I'll tell Mother I have to be away overnight on official business. Then I'll leave my car for a checkup and get in your car."

"Official business, eh? I'm waiting to be enlightened."

"Have you got all night?" She sounded

serious rather than playful, arousing his curiosity no end.

"Unfortunately, no. I still have patients I need to call before it gets any later. But next Saturday I want to hear it all."

"You may be sorry. Please don't let me hold you up any longer, Luca. I'm staying at the Badrutt's Palace Hotel."

He started the car again and drove to the center of the town. "A ton of journalists hang around there waiting for celebrities to show up and make their day. One sight of Princess Baldasseri with a local will create a frenzy."

"Which is why I'll ask you to drop me off at that next corner. I'll walk the rest of the way."

"I'll follow you in the car until I see you're safely inside."

"Don't worry about me. My bodyguard is always following me, and I carry this in my purse for protection." She pulled out a pocket-sized version of bear spray even though there weren't any.

She needed that kind of protection. "Whoa." Luca laughed. "If Alf Jr. had any idea." He pulled over to the curb.

Bella put it back in her purse with a smile and looked over at him. "I've had the most wonderful evening in ten years. Thank you from the bottom of my heart. You'll never know how much I've needed to see you for closure."

But Luca *did* know, having suffered from the same agony. He leaned across her to open the passenger door. Her fragrance assailed him. "I'll see you next Saturday." On their campout he'd tell her what happened to the letters.

She rolled those fabulous violet eyes. "We can hope, but after our history, there could be interference. I won't believe it until I see you again face-to-face."

He couldn't let her go like this, not after remembering what had happened ten years ago. "I'll give you a call if something untoward comes up."

She placed her hand in his, he lightly touched his lips to the top of it. Releasing her fingers, he continued, "If both our phones are stolen for some inexplicable reason, we know where to find each other." He sat back, loving it that he could just look at her after all these years.

"*Arrivederci*, Luca."

Once she crossed the street, every male in sight watched her as she headed for the famous old hotel. He kept driving and heard wolf whistles until she'd disappeared inside, then he headed for his apartment.

After returning some calls to patients, he opened his storage unit and took inventory of his camping equipment. Most weekends he stayed up in the mountains. He had a double sleeping bag, but would buy a new one for her. Everything else he had on hand. The question now was how to stand it until he saw her again next Saturday.

At noon on Wednesday, Luca went to the sporting goods store he often frequented, this time to check out sleeping bags engineered for women. He found a quilted rectangular bag that could turn into a down-filled blanket. Bella would love it. He carried it down the aisle to the sales guy at the counter who usually waited on him.

"Hey, Doc. Nice choice in blue," he commented and wrapped it up. "For your girlfriend?"

Luca gave him his credit card. "For a friend."

"Yeah?" The other guy's eyes twinkled as he put in the numbers and handed it back to him. "Have fun."

He walked out to the car with his purchase and headed for the office. When he pulled into his space, he carried the bag inside just to keep it safe in case someone broke into his car. It had happened before when someone was looking for drugs.

Adele eyed him immediately. "Your father is in your office. He's been waiting for you," she said in an accusatory manner.

"Thank you."

He strode down the hall and entered his office. His dark-haired father with silver showing at the temples glanced at the purchase. "It looks like you've been shopping at Wasescha Sport. I thought we had a lunch date."

Luca put the bag in the corner by his desk. "So we did, Papa. I forgot it was Wednesday. I'm sorry."

"Your mother and I hope you'll come over for dinner tonight."

"I will if I can." He knew his father would ask him what he'd done on the weekend.

The older man sat forward. Lines creased his face. "What's going on, son?"

"I'm sorry. I'm afraid I've been preoccupied with a couple of my patients."

"Maybe a particular woman too?"

"That sounds like something you know about that I don't."

His father grimaced. "According to Adele, you left the office with one last Friday after work. I've the feeling Adele has been hoping you would ask her out. I didn't know you were seeing anyone special."

Luca sat back in his chair. The receptionist had taken one look at Bella, whose beauty was exceptional along with everything else, and had understood that she was outmatched. It was possible she'd recognized Princess Baldasseri. With his parent giving him the steely eye, he'd had enough.

"Father? You know how much I love you and Mother, how grateful I am for all you've done for me. But it's obvious you've forgotten I'm a grown man living my own life. Please understand I have to follow my own path."

The older Dr. Torriani scowled and got to his feet. "There's something you're not telling me."

"But I *have* told you," he said, barely

concealing his rage, "and now there's a patient waiting for me."

"This isn't the end of our conversation."

It was as far as Luca was concerned. "I'll let Mamma know if I'm free tonight."

His father left the office like a bear coming out of hibernation. In a sense, Luca felt like he'd come out of one that had lasted a decade. Certain comments Bella had made ran through his mind. He'd always loved this daring side of Bella, but feared it could cause real damage with her mother.

We're both over twenty-one and in charge of our own lives. We're free to live the way we want.

Yes, they were, even if it meant real trouble. He was ready for it, and Bella seemed willing.

Elated for the weekend coming up, he sailed through the rest of his workweek. As Saturday dawned, he was up with the birds and left for Scuol in jeans and a T-shirt. When he saw a creamy Kimera Lancia that had to be Bella's parked at Lishana's Garage, a sense of homecoming almost overpowered him.

Luca drove in and stopped near the side

of the building, but he didn't shut off the engine. Through his rearview mirror he watched Bella, also clad in jeans, T-shirt and hiking boots, walk around holding a small duffel bag. She'd put her hair into a braid and wore a baseball cap. The cap brought back dozens of memories.

He reached over to open the passenger door and put the bag in the back seat before she slid in. "Hurry and drive away before Dizo sees you."

Luca took off. Dizo had been Luca's mentor. Now the master mechanic ran the garage. No guy was a bigger gossip and she knew it. Luca headed for the road that led up into the mountains.

She looked back. "I think we escaped before he realized what was happening."

He flashed her a sideward glance. "I thought we'd escaped the evil eye last Friday night. But thanks to the receptionist, this week my father let me know he'd heard I'd left the office with an unknown woman. He wanted to know what was going on. Knowing how his mind works, he has to be thinking you and I reconnected at the wedding."

She groaned. "I'm way ahead of you there. Mother expected I would stay with her and the grandparents at the hotel in Bern after the wedding. But Francesca asked me to stay at her parents' home. Mother couldn't say no, but she didn't like it.

"And earlier this morning her maid saw me slip out with my duffel bag. I'll be facing an interrogation tomorrow, considering I'm supposed to be leaving on official business."

"I'm afraid we can't elude palace security, Bella. We're being followed and you know it."

"I do, and today I don't care."

"Neither do I." They smiled at each other. She looked adorable in that same baseball cap of the Swiss Alpine Club she used to wear years ago. "How was the party for your grandfather?"

"Mother invited their best friends, a married couple. I'm sure you've heard of them, Prince and Princess Renaldo, my friend Constanza's parents. She came with them. We ate out on the terrace. I gave him a 1560 Romansh translation of the New Testament. I had to hunt for a copy."

"I bet he was thrilled."

"I think so. He and Nonna are deeply religious, but in a good way."

"What do you mean by that?"

"In a word, they don't judge people."

Luca sat forward. "That makes them very good people. The world needs more of them. Now I want to talk about that business you're in that brought you to my office in Saint Moritz."

"First you need to understand about the pain I suffered over the separation from you a decade ago. It affected my whole life. Finally I made an appointment to see my lifelong physician, Dr. Pendergast. He sat me down and asked me to tell him my whole story from the beginning in order to understand my depression. When I finished, he had one suggestion for me. I'll quote him.

"Bella? Since you'll never be able to be with Luca again, never be able to say you're sorry and help him, then find a way to help others who suffer from a similar injury. It could ease this pain of guilt you've been carrying around far too long to be healthy."

To hear this sadness coming from Bella ignited Luca's anger. His father had destroyed all her letters where she'd poured out her pain. How did Luca get beyond it?

All those years he'd thought she'd lost total interest in him. After they'd been manipulated and permanently separated by their families, he hadn't realized that Bella had gone through the same horrific kind of trauma he'd experienced over the years. All of it had been so unnecessary, even criminal in his eyes.

Yet you didn't do anything about it, Luca. You didn't fight for her. No matter your reasons for holding back, you didn't go after her. You've been a coward and unworthy of her. But not any longer.

"Bella? There's something you need to know. I only found out about it last week. My father intercepted all the letters you wrote to me the second they came to house. He ripped up every one of them."

"What?"

"It's true."

"How could your father, or any father, do that? Why was he so intent on keeping us apart?"

"I don't know, but I'm going to find out."

"You were right, Luca. Your father and my mother made a formidable team."

"*Formidable* is the right word. More than ever, I'm convinced that the help your Dr. Pendergast gave you makes him one brilliant doctor, Bella."

"He's wonderful and his advice helped me get through the last year with new purpose. Since there was no place for my marketing skills at our family's timber office, I decided to do what my mother had been begging me to do."

"Charity work?" By now they were climbing higher in the mountains above the palace, and she had him riveted.

"Yes. That's the proper job for a princess to do. After a lot of contemplation, I did research on children with all kinds of physical disadvantages because of accidents and injuries like yours."

"The need for help in that department is staggering, as you quickly found out."

She nodded. "I'm no doctor like you, but for once I felt that a royal *could* be useful."

Oh, Bella... "How did you get started? When? I can't even imagine it."

A sigh escaped her lips. "I couldn't either. It was like eating an elephant one bite at a time. About a year ago I decided to contact various service organizations around Graubunden and Eastern Switzerland first. I spent hours on the phone finding the right people to talk to.

"One man in Arosa asked me to meet him. After I explained what I wanted to do, he got excited. I told him I didn't want the Baldasseri name mentioned, only that I wanted to help. I went with Alectrona Cossu and it stuck."

Luca just shook his head. "I'm in awe of your industry and perseverance."

"He put me in touch with some health care workers and came up with a list of two children—one needed a hand, the other an arm. I investigated the cost of a prosthesis. The amount is astronomical to a poor family with little or no insurance. On a burst of inspiration, I wrote letters to my family's friends asking for a donation to help those two children.

"To my joy, money came in. The thought of an injured child had touched their heartstrings. When those two children had undergone their operations and were functioning, I sent the donors some before-and-after pictures to thank them for their contributions."

Her eyes filled with tears. "You'll never know how much it meant to receive letters from the donors who were thrilled to have helped. What else could they do, they asked. My experimental project had been a success and gave me more reason to keep on going. I'm not saying that what I did made my pain over you go away miraculously, but I've been happier."

"You're one remarkable woman." Bella had always been kind and generous, but this side of her proved she had a heart of pure gold. He loved her beyond life itself.

"Not remarkable. I just wanted to get rid of my guilt over what I did to you ten years ago. Every time a child is helped, it takes a little more of that guilt away."

He groaned. "You've paid for a crime you didn't commit a thousand times over. Let it go now, Bella."

"Being with you again has helped me more than you know. I consider it a job now, one that's worthy."

"I'm so glad it's fulfilling you, Bella,"

Luca sighed. "When you came to my office, you mentioned a boy in need…?"

"Yes. One eleven-year-old named Hasper Bazzell. He lost his left leg below the knee a month ago when he took the tractor out to the field. His father had forbidden him ever to touch it. He was years too young to drive it." She choked up and tears trickled down her cheeks. "His father had died earlier and he was trying to do a man's work when it tipped over and the accident occurred. The mother has little money and doesn't know what to do to help her son."

Bella's compassion for the boy touched his heart. Luca was humbled by what she'd told him. "I'm impressed beyond words and want to be able to help your cause."

"I didn't tell you this so you would feel obligated, Luca."

"You think I don't know that?" he emoted. "We're coming to our favorite spot by the river to camp." So far he hadn't seen any other hikers or campers. They had the place to themselves. "Later tonight we'll talk more about this boy."

CHAPTER FIVE

IT MAY HAVE been ten years, but for Bella it was like yesterday the minute they parked and started to set up their camp. They both knew their duties. Luca got busy putting up their three-man tent. The sight of his tall, rock-hard body driving in the stakes made it difficult for her to concentrate on her job.

She reached for the cinder blocks he kept in the trunk to form a small keyhole firepit on the spot where they'd made one many times before. After arranging them, she carried the kindling and placed it inside. The grate and charcoal could come out later when they decided to cook their dinner. By now their tent had been erected and Luca had taken their duffel bags inside.

"Let there be light." Bella walked in with the lanterns, then stopped in her tracks. "What's this?" His double sleeping bag had been placed on one side, but there was something new and blue on the other side beneath the small window with the netting.

His enticing smile made her body tremble. "*Your* sleeping bag."

"It's so plush! I brought my old one, but it doesn't compare to this." She sank down on it. "Ooh, down filled. Luca?" She looked up into those glinting green eyes. "You didn't need to do this."

"I wanted to."

"This is so fun I think I must be dreaming." More than anything in this world she wanted him to join her on the plump sleeping bag. She had to remember it was a miracle he'd even agreed to spend this day and night with her, but just being with him again now was no longer enough for her. Possibly he felt nothing deeper for her beneath the surface but that's what she had to find out on this trip.

"Come on, Bella. What do you say we visit the Garden of Eden, then come back and fish for our dinner? I'm hungry for perch."

She got to her feet. "That or trout sounds wonderful!" She tossed her cap on the sleeping bag, not wanting to hike with it. Once out of the tent, he zipped the entrance closed. Before locking up the car, he pulled out water bottles already filled for them. They hooked them to their belts. Now they were ready.

Between the mountain peaks and birdsong, Bella felt they'd come to the land of enchantment. The fragrant scent of pine intoxicated her. If she only had this one weekend with him, she would treasure it forever.

They started to forge their own trail through a meadow full of thousands of yellow flowers that grew on these mountains. "Isn't this the most beautiful sight you ever saw?" she cried, moving her hands carefully over the tops of some.

"Beautiful," came the deep response.

Bella glanced up and discovered him studying her. *Oh, Luca*—what was he thinking? She would give anything if he'd tell her what was really going on inside him. There was a rightness in them being together like this again. He had to be feeling it too! But there was this great silence on his part. Again she was determined to find out if she was the only one in love.

They reached a forested area where they came upon a little family of stone marten foxes with white and gray fur darting around. Luca paused and took a picture with his camera. "Cute, aren't they?" he whispered.

"Delightful beyond anything."

"Isn't it interesting they're the predators of the forest these days, not the bears."

"It's sad isn't it," she murmured. "Vincenzo told me a bear did make it over a mountain pass from Italy into the Biosphere reserve years ago. They're monitoring it. I hope more are allowed to stay."

"We're lucky your brother and the conservation board are watching over the environment here."

She finished taking a picture that caught one of the foxes and Luca's profile. "Do you think your father knows?"

"I'm sure he does, but all the good Vincenzo does won't remove my father's prejudice against royalty. It's his flaw and I no longer care."

Bella wished she hadn't mentioned his father. After drinking some water, they left the forest and entered another meadow.

Above it they would come to their favorite place.

Halfway there she noticed a bird cruising high in the sky. "Look, Luca—am I crazy or is that a bearded vulture?"

Luca had seen it too. "You have a sharp eye, Bella. That reddish color is a dead giveaway."

They both took pictures before he snapped one of her. Thrilled he'd done that, she moved faster to reach their favorite spot. Ten years had produced more grassy undergrowth and the tree branches above them had intertwined into a virtual solid roof forming their own cathedral.

They walked around underneath. "I don't see any sign of the hares, Luca."

"After ten years they've probably moved on to paradise."

"I think they must have been very happy here."

"I know I was," he admitted. "Do you remember once telling me and Vincenzo that you wished we lived right here?"

Heat swamped her cheeks. "I said a lot of foolish things."

"Not foolish," he came back. "I felt the

same away. No rules or restrictions up here. No one to tell us what we had to do."

"Free," she murmured.

"Exactly. There's no feeling like it."

"That was how it was for me…before—"

"Before our fantasy world disappeared?" he interjected.

She took a deep breath. "I don't think it was such a good idea to come up here. The memories still hurt too much. Let's go back to the river and do some fishing." Her gaze swerved to his. "Did you bring your fishing license?"

"I brought one for both of us."

"You always think of everything." *There's no one like you, Luca Torriani.*

"Actually, I forgot the fishing nets you and Vincenzo used to take when you couldn't sneak poles out of the palace."

She laughed and started walking out into the late afternoon sun.

He caught up to her. "I want to hear more about your charity. How many children have you helped already?"

She looked over her shoulder at him. "Probably thirty-five, but there are so many more. They all need help from someone who has suffered the same way you did."

He shook his head. "My suffering ended in a few weeks. After I went to college in Ohio, my father talked to me about becoming an allergist so I could work with him. I told him I thought I might like to be an orthopedic surgeon like the doctor who operated on me."

"How did that go over?"

"Papa fought me on it. He gave me all the reasons why being a surgeon would be a bad choice. He said I would suffer burnout, depression and face malpractice suits. The education would cost too much when it wasn't worth it."

She eyed him. "Yet I bet he was thankful for the surgeon who fixed your leg."

Luca smiled. "*I* certainly was, and I reminded him of the same thing. For once he had no answer. Later I had to do rehabilitation and was sent to a sports medicine doctor for a few sessions of therapy. I liked his approach and he talked to me about other careers as a doctor I'd never considered.

"When I got into medical school and had to make a decision, you know what I did.

My father wasn't thrilled about it. He never liked most of my decisions."

"You *did* become a doctor. Surely that had to satisfy him."

"To some degree. A doctor is still a doctor, just like a princess is still a princess, even if you don't want to be considered one."

No, she didn't, and she'd give anything if he'd drop the subject.

They reached camp and Luca pulled their fly rods out of the trunk. While she started the fire so they could cook their catch, he called to her. "What fly do you want?"

"Guess!"

He didn't have to and put on her favorite.

In a few minutes she hurried over to him and inspected it. "My mayfly nymph. It always brings me luck."

Luca grinned. "Don't I know it. You're the best fisherwoman I've ever been with."

One brow lifted. "Is that a *long* list, Dr. Torriani?"

"Probably not as long as the list of fisher princes you've entertained over the last ten years."

Fisher princes? A caustic laugh burst

from her as she turned to him with that crushing hurt in her heart. "Just for tonight, could we be Luca and Bella who went through high school together, but never even got to attend the graduation dance?"

The pain in her voice echoed his own pain and ripped him raw. "Come on, Bella. First one to get a strike cooks the dinner."

Luca ran down to the bank ahead of her. She squealed and hurried after him. For the next half hour they fished their favorite spots. Plenty of fish filled the water this far upstream. Bella was a picture playing with her fly rod like it was a lasso ready to ensnare a bull at a rodeo with precision.

To his surprise they both caught a large trout at the same time and let out shouts of excitement. He walked over and took her fish off the hook. "Since it's a tossup, I'll clean them and bring them to you to cook."

Within twenty minutes he'd set up their chairs at the small camping table and she'd cooked their fish to perfection. With fruit and a pasta salad he'd made and put in the cooler, he'd never had a better meal in his life. Bella was the unique ingredient that made tonight surreal.

By the time they'd finished eating and had done the cleanup, it had grown dark. She went to the tent with a lantern to get ready for bed. He locked everything in the trunk before approaching.

"Knock, knock." He waited at the entrance expecting her to unzip the opening.

Instead, he heard, "Have you forgotten the password?"

"No, but I wasn't sure if you remembered." Vincenzo had thought it up years ago when they were young and needed one in case of an emergency. *Winky.* He'd derived it from the name Arnold Winkelried, who'd been a legendary hero in sixteenth-century Swiss history.

"You go first," she challenged him.

A smile broke out on his face. "I don't think so."

"Luca—"

"It's okay you've forgotten. I'll just sleep in the car."

In a panic she cried out, "Winky!" and undid the zipper.

Nothing could have brought him more satisfaction. He couldn't help laughing. Luca loved it that she ended up laughing with him.

Was there a woman more gorgeous than Bella standing there in the lamp light, her blond hair gleaming? She wore a black short-sleeved top with a Geneve-Suisse logo and Red Cross flag on the front. The black-and-white-plaid bottoms completed the outfit.

He wanted to crush her in his arms, but another prince would be in her destiny before long. "Do I need another password to come inside?"

Her eyes glowed a deep lavender. "Not a password, Luca. All I ask is that you remove that defensive armor and be the guy I knew before the avalanche. Is there no way under heaven you can look at me like I'm a normal woman? Or is this an excuse because there really *is* an important woman in your life? Believe me I would understand and be so happy for you."

Her earnestness could be his undoing. "Shall we go inside and get comfortable while we talk?"

"Of course."

He followed her in and zipped up the opening. "Close your eyes while I pull on some sweats."

She'd already climbed inside her bag. "I never used to."

He smiled. "Then enjoy the show."

"I saw many a sight when we were all together."

Bella. "I'm sorry to hear about it and don't think I want to know more."

Her laughter resounded in the tent.

Extinguishing his lantern, Luca only took a second to remove his jeans and put on his camouflage sweats. He left his boots on and subsided on his sleeping bag before turning toward her. The lantern next to her was still on and bathed her in a soft, beautiful aura.

"Your mother must have been inspired to call you Alectrona. The picture I see in my mind of her looks a lot like you, even if your hair is in a braid. Amazing."

"I never had one when we were young. My hair wasn't long enough. I liked it short, but mother felt it wasn't becoming on me, so I had to let it grow out. Yours hasn't changed."

"I grew it longer in Columbus."

She smiled. "Did you like it?"

"My parents came to visit and hated it."

"Why didn't you keep it long?"

"You never change, Bella. The truth is, my hair isn't curly and it kept getting in my eyes."

She chuckled and propped herself on one elbow. "Do you have a picture?"

"Somewhere."

"I'd like to see it."

"Why?"

Her violet eyes searched his. "I want to catch up on the ten years I missed. Do you realize that except for vacations, the three of us probably saw each other every day growing up?"

Yes, he did, and was trying desperately to forget. "We were quite the triumvirate."

"That's right! Vincenzo was Caesar, you were Pompey, and I was Crassus. You should have been Caesar. In real life my brother never wanted to be king, but I was afraid it would hurt his feelings if I voted for *you* to be our leader."

"That's what I like about you, Bella. Not only are you a flatterer, you're a loving sister, loyal to the end."

"Then why did I get the name Crassus?"

"That was easy. Like a politician, you defied the powers that be and had enough pocket money for us when we ran out of ours."

She fell back against her pillow. "Money means little when you're not truly happy. How's that for the world's worst cliché."

He felt her pain. "What kind of a statement is that?"

"A true one." She rolled on her side once more. "Is your life making sense to you? I'm not talking about your being a doctor. I'm talking about you as a man."

"That's a loaded question," he teased.

"I'm Crassus, remember?" She sat straight up. "Take off your helmet for one minute and look at me. Tell me what you think your life would have been like if I weren't a royal and we were a normal couple. When the avalanche was shooting down the mountain, you gave me a swift kiss and said, 'I love you, too, Bella. Always will.'"

He reached for a bottle of water and drank. "I meant it, Bella. But you were a princess. We were teenagers, a stage we had to outgrow to become sensible adults."

"That statement sounds like one from our parents you've had memorized for a decade."

"At that particular time, it had to become my mantra."

She got up on her knees. "No one knows that better than I do. But now that we're all grown up and have become reacquainted, the rules have changed. I'm old enough to be with the man I want."

His chest tightened. "If not with Prince Antonio, then another prince."

"No. That's my mother's expectation. Since seeing you at my brother's wedding, I've rediscovered what it means to be with you. No one else will ever satisfy me." Tears trickled down her flushed cheeks. "I can't speak for you. If you haven't married because you haven't found the right woman yet, then that's one thing. But if you feel the same way I feel and don't want to be with anyone else but me, then I have a proposal."

His body started to tingle. He got to his feet. "What are you saying?"

"I'm no longer a princess. That part of my life is over no matter what lies ahead. I've already written to King Leonardo, telling him I've renounced my title to live the life of a commoner."

"You've done *what*?" Luca cried.

"It's true."

"But Bella—don't you realize that throwing your birthright away could be disastrous for you in ways you can't possibly imagine?"

"I don't know. I guess I'll find out."

"What if he won't grant it?"

"If he doesn't present it to the parliament, it doesn't matter. I've relinquished my title and told my mother. Vincenzo was allowed to marry a commoner, so why should I be denied the same right? I'm younger and further down the line of succession considering they want to raise a family. I plan to live a free life from here on out."

Maybe he was dreaming all this.

"All you have to do is say you want me too. Naturally if you can't because I'm not the one, it won't change a thing. If you decide you want me, we can be together any way you'd like for as long as you want."

"Bella—you don't know what you're saying."

"It's up to you," she kept on talking. "You set the parameters, *if* that's what you desire. I'll do whatever it takes to see you, meet you wherever, whenever you say. We'll work around your medical practice schedule. We could even *live* together if you wanted to. I'd do anything for you. It all depends on whether you're on fire for me too."

Live together... "Bella—can you hear yourself?"

"I've been thinking these thoughts for years!"

"Stop! You're going to regret what you are saying. It's up to me to protect you from yourself. Don't you see that?" he cried.

"Oh, I see all right." Tears gushed down her hot cheeks. "It appears my news hasn't set you on fire. I have my answer."

"What answer?"

"You don't feel the same way I do. You don't believe I can manage my affairs on my own. Well, that's too bad. Under the circumstances I'd like you to drive me back to town right now rather than stay the rest of the night."

She got out of the sleeping bag and stood up. "Let's pack up. I'm ready to go."

Luca watched her gather her duffel bag. Was she already regretting her decision to give up her title?

Suddenly she spun around. "After being

with you again, that painful period of not acting on my feelings has come to a permanent end, Luca. When I go home, I'm going to move out of the palace and get an apartment with the money I've earned working.

"I'll get a job and continue to do charity work. As of today I intend to live my life as Bella Baldasseri from here on out—a normal citizen of Scuol with all the parts and passions of every child born into the world."

He couldn't believe what he was hearing. "I'll take you back, but I hope you won't be regretting your decision, Bella. What you're doing is like being born again. You don't know what you could be facing."

"That's the whole idea, Luca. Born again and free. Are you coming, or do I have to hike down the mountain? Remember I've got my bear spray."

He tossed her the car keys. "Go out to the car and wait for me."

CHAPTER SIX

BELLA HAD DONE it now. She sat in the car and waited for him to join her while he packed up the tent. Since seeing him at the wedding, she'd been the one to follow him out to the taxi, not the other way around. She'd flown to Saint Moritz and had shown up at his office unannounced. The campout had been her idea, not his. Worst of all, *she'd* been the one to suggest they could live together.

Once again, she'd thrown caution to the wind to entice him, praying he would reveal his true feelings. Well, she knew his true feelings now! Worse, she'd committed the cardinal sin. *A man liked to do the chasing.* But she'd taken the risk, and she'd found out he wasn't in love with her.

Still, she wasn't sorry. She would call Nonna Caderina and tell her she'd given

Luca the ultimate test. And now he was taking her home because there was nothing more to say.

It hurt that Luca couldn't do the honest thing and simply reject her like he would a normal woman who'd proposed something he didn't desire. That was because he would always see her as an untouchable princess running around with him and Vincenzo.

The three of them had grown up in their own halcyon universe, but it was ten years later now. At this point she was the only one left in it. Both he and Vincenzo had moved on and were leading their own lives. Why did it take her until the age of twenty-six to grasp that fact?

Full of shame over such emotional immaturity, she stared out the window as he drove them down the mountain to the back of the palace. The guard stood at attention at the entrance. She'd send for her car at the station in the morning.

When Luca pulled to a stop, she grabbed her duffel bag from the back seat and got out of the car. "Thank you for the great campout. Being with you since the wedding has allowed me to express my sorrow for what happened ten years ago. You've been wonderful to let me relive some choice memories from our past. God bless you in the future, Luca Torriani."

She walked inside past the guard. If pain could burn you alive, she'd be ashes by now.

Once she reached her suite, she dropped the bag and ran for her bedroom. When she dived for her bed, her baseball cap fell on the floor.

"Bella?"

She turned over.

Her well-dressed mother picked up her cap and put it on the dresser. "We need to have a talk." She sat on one of the upholstered chairs and crossed her legs.

"What's wrong?"

"Several things. I've been on the phone with Mamma's caregiver in Sardinia. She has developed a bad cold."

"I thought as much. I talked to her the other day, and her cough was much worse. I'm very worried about her."

"If she doesn't get better in a few days, I want you to go with me to see her, Bella. You'll have to plan a trip around your charity duties."

"Of course. Poor Nonna. What a terrible life she has lived since Nonno died. Of course I'll go with you. I love her."

"As I said, she's just one of my concerns. Considering you've been camping rather than carrying out official charity business, I should be thankful you came home before the weekend was over."

Bella took several breaths in succession. She'd known this was coming. "It's Luca you need to thank. You and his father did such a fantastic job on him, he's been programmed like one of the robots made by Constanza's family business. He's such a good little boy, he returned me untouched and pure as the gold from our family's King Midas Mine."

Her mother's brows furrowed. "I can't believe you're speaking to me this way."

Trying to tamp down her anger, Bella got to her feet. "I can't believe that you and Papa colluded with Dr. Torriani to permanently separate Luca and me after the avalanche. That move of his to Saint Moritz was pure genius."

She averted her eyes and clasped her hands tightly. "Did Vincenzo tell you?"

"No. *You* did. He's just a robot who took orders from the three of you. Luca and I figured it out for ourselves when we saw each other at Vincenzo's wedding."

"So, you *did* get together…"

"Several times since then actually, and you know it."

"What about Prince Antonio?"

"What about him?"

Her mother muttered something unintelligible, then said, "I forbad Vincenzo to invite Luca to the wedding, but he disobeyed me."

"That was probably the only time in his life he went against your wishes. Except, of course, for choosing Francesca for his bride before you learned the truth about Valentina's problems." She moved closer to her mother. "How could you expect him to obey your wishes when Luca has been his best friend for years?"

Her mother's features hardened. "You know why we—"

"I know exactly," Bella interrupted her while she undid her braid. "I *was* Princess Baldasseri who would have to marry the right prince. Those are the words you spoke to me at the hospital that night. Thankfully I'm no longer a princess."

Those blue eyes stared hard at her. "It's your destiny, Bella."

"Afraid not, Mamma. Phone King Leonardo if you want to hear that I rescinded my title."

She jumped to her feet. "That couldn't be true!"

"You'll find out, and you ought to stop obsessing about my future."

"You're being ridiculous."

"It's not ridiculous, just honest. The only man I've ever loved or will love is Luca. But of his own free will and no one else's edicts, Luca never wanted to marry me. If that had been his desire, he would have come after me years before now and talked me into running away with him." During tonight Bella had come to recognize the real truth of his feelings.

She walked over to her mother and kissed her cheek. "I love you more than you know. Because you're a princess and want me to have the same life as yours, I understand what motivated you and Papa back then. I hope you love me enough now that I'm a commoner."

A gasp came from her parent.

"I'll continue to do my charity work, Mamma, but beyond that I'm going to live a free life."

A tragic look crossed over her mother's face. For once she appeared at a loss for words.

"While I'm in the shower, why don't you phone Luca's father and let him know that the problem has been forever solved. Maybe then he'll stop trying to run his son's love life, let alone everything else. I'll say it one more time. Dr. Torriani's worries are over and so are *yours*."

She went in the bathroom and shut the door. It wasn't until the water was streaming down her head and face that tears of anguish poured from her eyes.

Bella cried herself to sleep that night, but by the morning, she'd wiped her tears away and had made a decision.

After college in England, Vincenzo had moved out of the palace for five years before their father died. It had given him the freedom to enjoy being a bachelor. Bella wanted that kind of freedom for a myriad of reasons. She could enjoy any man she wanted, or no man at all.

All she had to do was get on the computer and find a two-bedroom apartment here in Scuol. She'd make one room into an office to run her charity business. That way she could invite people to meet with her when they could come.

Bella had some savings from her former job. She also had a car. Naturally she'd visit her mother and grandparents often and stay in touch. Of course, she couldn't do anything about her mother hiring security to keep an eye on her.

Pleased with her decision to become her own person, she dressed and went into her study to get on the computer. Two hours later she left her mother a message that she'd gone out but would be back by dinner. Starving at this point, she drove to a local drive-through for a meal before checking out the furnished apartments in Scuol.

She remembered that Vincenzo had rented a great condo at a location called The

Spruces. Each condo was a separate home with a veranda and a view of the mountains. Bella had loved visiting him when she'd come home from Geneva for the rare weekend. He'd just bought Karl. She fell in love with his puppy. Those were joyous memories.

Bella wished she could rent the one Vincenzo had lived in, but now they were privately owned. That was okay. Within an hour she found a furnished two-bedroom rental on the first floor she liked at the Silvretta Lodge. She didn't want to climb stairs. It was perfect and had been modernized with simple furnishings. The landlady couldn't have been more accommodating. After living in a sumptuous palace, it was like a breath of fresh air.

Tonight at dinner Bella would tell the family her plans and move in on Saturday. Hopefully her grandmother would recover from the pneumonia and they wouldn't have to leave for Sardinia quite yet. Before long Bella would be inviting Vincenzo and Francesca over for *fondue au fromage* to celebrate. It would be the beginning of a new triumvirate that didn't include Pompey.

* * *

Bella got up early Saturday morning and dressed in jeans and a yellow crew neck top. She put her hair in a French twist so she wouldn't have to deal with it. Once she'd eaten breakfast, she was ready to go.

After a dozen trips to her car with her things, she left for her apartment. Rain had been forecast for today and the temperature had dropped. If she hurried, she'd miss the downpour.

The nice thing about a furnished apartment meant she didn't need furniture. Only her clothes, toiletries, a few items for the kitchen she'd already bought and everything for her office. A new chapter in her life was beginning that didn't include Luca.

She pulled in her parking stall at the side of the complex and turned off the engine. Ready to get busy, she grabbed the bag with her toiletries lying on the front seat. But when she opened the car door, a tall, hard male body prevented her from getting out.

Bella looked up into glittering, jewel-like green eyes she'd thought never to see again. It was a good thing he prevented her from standing up or she would have fainted dead away on the cement.

"Put your head down and take a deep breath, Bella." She did his bidding. Luca's deep voice kept her from losing consciousness. He rubbed the back of her neck. The touch of his fingers ignited her senses, bringing her back to life. She finally lifted her head. "Better now?"

"I can breathe again." She sat up straighter and gripped the steering wheel.

"That's something, but don't bother trying to get out yet." She heard the old familiar amusement in his tone. "The last time this happened, the snow buried us alive."

Bella struggled to comprehend what was happening. "How—"

"Vincenzo is back from their honeymoon. I was ready to phone you when he called. Your mother told him you renounced your title and planned to move to this apartment today," he broke in, reading her thoughts. "Rather than phone you, I came right over."

She shook her head. "What would we do without Vincenzo, but you've made a wasted trip."

He shifted his weight, drawing her attention to his cropped denims and navy pullover. It was her favorite color on him. "The night of our campout, you proposed that we live together. After living twenty-eight years without hope that I could ever be with you, I drove home in shock trying to comprehend that you'd actually proposed we live together."

Bella could grant that what she'd said would have stunned him.

"On the drive back to Scuol, so many thoughts bombarded my mind, but foremost was the courage it took for you to consider turning your entire universe around for me. A part of me wanted to protect you from yourself before you went too far and regretted it."

"I don't need protecting, Luca."

"I realize that now." One dark brow lifted. "You said you'd do anything for me. It all depended on whether I was on fire for you."

"I did say that." Bella still clung to the steering wheel. She regretted those words now.

"I'm on fire for you, Bella. I've never been

anything else. I love you with every breath in my body. You've always known how I felt."

She threw her head back to look up at him. "No, I don't, Luca. You drove me back to the palace without a word. Considering that I laid my life on the line for you, that was an amazing response for a man on fire."

He leaned closer. "After the night of our campout, I had many things to work out before I could come to you with my answer. It was my mistake not to stay in the tent and love us both into oblivion forever."

"No, it wasn't a mistake. You've never been spontaneous with me or come running to me, Luca. Only that one time on the mountain when I was in danger."

"Bella—" he whispered in a tortured voice.

"Your silence has been a good thing and gave me my answer. I've had this week to decide I like the idea of being on my own and independent. It's going to be fun to live the normal life of a commoner like millions of other women. But thank you for finally getting back to me, even if it wasn't necessary. Now I need to unpack. I have a lot of work to do."

"Bella—I realize my silence has condemned me. I've done everything wrong and am begging you to forgive me. I love you beyond anything in existence."

"I don't doubt you love me in your own way. We have a unique history. But we're not the right match and time has proven it."

"Nothing has been proven, Bella. Give me the chance to convince you we're meant to be together. Do you feel strong enough to drive?"

She blinked. "Why are you asking me that?"

"My car is parked a few feet away. When you're able, I want you to follow me in your car. We don't have far to go, and then I'll explain why I don't want you to move into this apartment. There's so much I need to say to you."

"There you go again, putting off answers. It's your modus operandi."

"Please, Bella. If we leave now, we might beat the rain."

"I'm sorry, but my plans are set."

"You don't mean that."

Since he refused to go away, she started the car. He stepped away far enough for her to back out of her stall. Right now she needed sustenance in order to follow through with her resolve. A cup of coffee at the local drive-through would help. The rain started falling.

After her stop, she drove back to her apartment in a real downpour. She was still trembling from the encounter with Luca. The second she parked and got out of the car, she was caught around the waist from behind and let out a cry.

"Since you're no longer a princess, and I'm a normal man, I'm going to treat you like the normal woman you've always wanted to be. This is how we do it."

"No, Luca—" she cried out as he picked her up in his arms and carried her to his car. He ensconced her in the passenger seat and shut her door. Then he walked around and got behind the wheel.

"You want answers, *bellissima*? No more inaction. You're going to get them."

He drove down the road past the garage where he'd worked. When they reached The Spruces, he turned in and wound through the trees. It was like déjà vu after he pulled in the driveway.

"This is the condo my brother rented."

"A long time ago."

Luca parked the car and came around for Bella. He moved fast and had already unlocked the front door of the condo. She had no choice but to sweep past him, brushing the rain off her arms.

He walked in the living room for a throw and put it around her shoulders, squeezing them gently. "It's chilly all of a sudden. I'll turn up the heat. In fact, I could use a cup of coffee. I made a pot before coming to your apartment. Maybe you'd like another one."

"I want to go back to my apartment."

"Not until I've given you my full answer. Come in the kitchen and sit down."

She followed him and sat down at the table, still reacting to the feel of his touch. Bella had been in here before, but these furnishings were different. "Is my brother letting you stay in his condo?"

Luca brought each of them a mug of hot liquid and sat down across from her. "I don't suppose you know the story about this place. While I was in high school working at the garage, I would pass The Spruces.

I thought it would be fun to live in one of the rentals and told Vincenzo.

"He thanked me for the heads-up and agreed it would be a great place when we were both on our own. On one of my few visits home while I was in medical school, he called me."

"You flew in from Ohio?" To think he'd been here in Scuol and she'd known nothing…

"It was my mother's birthday. I wanted to surprise her. Your brother had just returned from London. He told me you were away or I would have used him to see you. We drove over here and looked at this condo for rent. The lucky dude put down money and moved in."

How incredible, and it had all been Luca's idea. "I remember how upset our parents were." She took another long swallow of coffee while she tried to absorb the astonishing information.

"We decided that after I finished my residency, I'd move into a rental here too and we'd lead the bachelor life. But due to my father, my plans had to change and then your father died."

"Yes. My mother begged my brother to come home."

"He knew she needed him. Around that time the group that owns The Spruces put the condos up for sale. I bought this one for an investment a year ago."

A cry escaped her lips. "But you live in Saint Moritz—"

"Not since four days ago."

"What?"

"That's one of the reasons you didn't hear from me until this morning."

She gripped the empty mug tighter, unable to process what she was hearing.

"More importantly, for over a year the Lemond Institute here in Scuol has been asking me to join them. If my father hadn't mapped out my life after leaving Germany, I would have started working with them. This week I accepted their offer and informed the medical group in Saint Moritz that I had left. I did all this so you and I can be together."

She stared at him in disbelief. "You're serious…"

"Will this start to convince you?" He reached in his pants pocket and pulled out a white gold band with two round gems the color of a purple violet. "I've loved you since we were children. Your eyes were this exact hue the first time I met you. You've always been the bride of my heart. Forgive me if it took this long for my answer. I had to put everything in place first because I not only want to live with you, I plan to *marry* you and live here with you."

"Marry?" she whispered in absolute shock. Her eyes filled with tears. "Oh, Luca… If only you'd told me this while we were out camping."

His brows furrowed. "You know why I didn't."

"But that's the difference between us. I was ready to throw everything away to be with you right then. Yet you didn't tell me you were in love with me or hold me all night. That was your choice, but since then I've undergone a change. Not my love for you, but my perspective about you."

"What do you mean?"

"Your entire life you've always been free to make choices when the time suited you. I've never had that luxury about anything until I rescinded my title. I like the freedom it's given me—the possibilities. I want to explore it for a little while. To marry you has always been my hopeless dream, but—"

"But now that it can be a reality, you're not sure," he finished for her in a deep, grating voice.

"No, it's not that. I'd just like the chance to live the life of a normal woman."

The light faded from his eyes. He put the ring back in his pocket. Bella felt him close up. Maybe this was the greatest mistake of her life. Maybe she wanted him to hurt the way she'd been hurting since the campout. All she knew was that she needed time to think about it.

"Don't let me keep you from your unpacking. I'll run you back to your apartment."

There was nothing more to be said. She got up and walked out to his car. During the short drive, the silence between them was deafening.

Once Bella had gone inside her apartment, Luca took off for their Garden of Eden. The pain was so excruciating, he didn't know how to deal with it. Clouds sat on the mountain while thunder cannonaded from peak to peak. The temperature had plummeted. By the time he got out of the car, he could hardly see where he was going. After putting on his backpack and bedroll, he hiked through the rain the rest of the way, plodding through wet underbrush.

Relieved the garden interior had remained dry, he spread out his bedroll and collapsed inside it. He lay there for hours, bombarded with self-recrimination for his lack of bravery at the campout. Why hadn't he told her he loved her and couldn't live without her? She'd just handed him his heart's desire. But it had sounded so impossible, he'd gone into shocked silence and had only himself to blame for her rejection.

Fool of fools, he'd kept her waiting a week for his answer. And then he'd charged over to her apartment on his time frame, not hers. Was it any wonder she didn't melt in his arms? After what he'd done, how could she believe anything he had to say?

Bella had been dictated to all her life. After getting rid of her title in a courageous move, she'd planned their campout and proposed to him on the spot. And what had he done? Wounded her to the core.

He groaned as the hours wore on and fear started to creep in. Love could be a fragile thing. Maybe her independent life would change the way she felt about him. She might even want her old royal role back.

Not if he had anything to say about it!

Luca shot straight up. He realized he needed to show her his love all over again before that could happen. Filled with resolve, he got to his feet. Until she accepted his heart and ring, he determined to give her a taste of what it was like to be a normal woman, desired by a normal man.

The rain had stopped by the time he reached town. He stopped at a floral shop and bought a dozen long-stemmed red roses before driving to her apartment at seven. Relieved to see her car still in its stall, he parked and approached her door. He could have used the doorbell, but knocked instead several times.

"Who is it?" she called out.

"Luca."

After a wait she finally opened the door looking gorgeous in a stunning blue dress.

In the background, a man he recognized as Prince Antonio sat on her sofa. Luca could hardly breathe. It felt like a slug in the gut to know she was with him. His eyes met hers as he handed her the box of flowers.

"I brought you a housewarming gift, something I should have done this morning. I've thought about everything you said. Since you're busy I'll call you tomorrow."

"I'm sorry, Luca, but I won't be available."

Luca could see a nerve throbbing in her throat. Was that because she would be spending more time with the Prince? He looked around, but didn't see a car that might belong to the other man. No doubt he'd flown in by helicopter and she'd picked him up in her car. "Sorry to have disturbed you. Another time, then. *Buna notg.*"

Luca knew that trying to win her back would be difficult, but he hadn't expected to see the Prince head-on. She'd wanted to be free. It looked like she was already making the most of it.

His jealousy worse than ever, he hurried back to his car and took off for his condo. Thank heaven the rest of his weekend would be busy filling in for two doctors away on a conference. Anything to deal with the pain.

No sooner had he parked his car in the driveway than Vincenzo phoned him.

"Did you find her?" his friend asked right off.

"I did." Luca apprised his friend of the situation. "She's enjoying her freedom with Prince Antonio tonight."

"Hang in there and give her time."

"I will." He had no choice. Bella was his whole life. He wouldn't give up. "Thanks for the moral support."

"Always. Just so you know, our *nonna* is ill, and Bella is worried."

"She told me. I'm so sorry."

"Me too. Call me anytime."

Luca hung up and went inside.

At six on Monday, he couldn't stand it any longer and called her to go out to dinner.

"I'm afraid I can't this evening. I have a ton of work."

Not to be daunted he said, "Then I'll bring you some pizza." He hung up before she could turn him down.

Within twenty minutes he stood at her door. She opened it wearing jeans and an oversize T-shirt. There was no Prince here tonight. Bella looked ravishing in anything, especially with her hair tousled. "You shouldn't have done this."

"Since I'm here, mind if I come in so we can eat while it's still hot? Afterward I can hang that picture you're holding before I leave."

She finally stood back so he could enter. So far, so good. He carried the box to the kitchen counter and looked around. "It looks like you've lived here a long time. I'm impressed." He opened the box. "Will you join me?" He sat on one of the stools and ate a couple of slices.

She put the framed picture against the wall. "This isn't going to work." The firmness in her tone twisted his gut.

"Because of Prince Antonio?"

"That's none of your business."

"Understood, but it's important you know I've come back to Scuol to live for the rest of my life. After talking to you on the campout, everything became crystal clear. I'm going to fight for us, Bella. If you're ready to give up on me, that's your call, but I'm never giving up on you. I'll let you get on with your evening now. I just wanted to make sure that was understood between us. Good night."

"Wait—" she called to him as he opened the door.

He turned to her. "What is it?"

"There is one problem that has me worried. I need your advice."

He heard concern in her voice. "What is it?"

"You know that boy Hasper Bazzell I told you about who lost the lower half of his leg?"

"Of course."

"His mother has said she doesn't want charity, but I felt something wasn't right so I phoned her today. We had a long talk. She said her son is afraid of everything. He won't talk to his school friends. He doesn't want to see any doctors and his depression is so bad, he just wants to stay in bed."

"That's not good."

"No. She's frantic and says raising money for him would be a waste. It's so sad. Because you're a doctor who has dealt with this kind of thing, do you have any ideas how I could talk to her and try to get through?"

"Why don't you let me try instead. Give me her number and I'll call tonight."

"I don't expect that, Luca."

"I know, but I'll do whatever it takes to help her son." *And hopefully show you I'll do anything for you, Bella.*

"That's very kind of you."

He added the number she gave him to his phone.

"Forgive me for being short with you earlier, Luca. I haven't even asked you how *your* work is going." It was the old Bella for a few minutes.

"Exactly as I had imagined."

"Are you glad about working at the Institute?"

"I am, but what is most important is that I'm home to stay. I'll get back to you after I've talked to Signora Bazzell. Get a good sleep."

The next night he phoned Bella, who picked up on the second ring. "Luca?" She sounded expectant, which was a plus.

"I have good news. I spoke with Signora Bazzell and told her I'd fly to Glarus to talk to her son. I've arranged it for Friday afternoon. My work will understand since

Hasper is going to be one of my cases on which I'm consulting."

"You're a miracle worker, Luca. When I last talked to her, she was so disheartened I didn't think anyone could get through to her. Come around to the back of the palace at noon on Friday. We'll fly to Glarus in the helicopter."

To fly with her was progress. He could make it to Friday after all.

He was still counting this blessing when he entered his condo. He showered and got in bed. For the next hour he answered half a dozen phone messages from his service. There was another message, this one from his father. It didn't require an answer.

There's no forgiveness for what you've done.

CHAPTER SEVEN

SUNNY SKIES PREVAILED over Glarus on Friday morning. Luca looked out the window of the helicopter at their approach. He liked the charming Swiss town of twelve thousand people located on the Linth River. The Alps surrounded it.

Before he and Bella had left the palace grounds, they made another phone call to Hasper's mother to finalize arrangements. She indicated that her boy refused to leave the house and meet them at the hospital. When Luca told Bella, she agreed with him they should rent a car and drive to the Bazzell farm.

"It's hard to believe that in a quaint, fairytale place like this, such a terrible tragedy happened to Hasper."

Luca reached for her hand without thinking and squeezed it. "Maybe this visit can turn his world around."

"I know you will find a way."

They followed directions up the hillside to the brown-and-white chalet. Signora Bazzell was waiting for them. She was a nice-looking, brown-haired mother probably thirty years of age trying to run the farm alone.

After introductions, she invited them inside and they went up the stairs. "Hasper is in his room."

"Does he know I'm coming?"

She nodded. "I told him a doctor wanted to visit him. That's all. He just turned away from me. I'm at my wit's end."

"Signorina Cusso and I would like to see him together." Bella knew all about the kind of guilt that played a big part in Hasper's problem. Her insight would be invaluable. "If you'll show us to his room, we'll introduce ourselves and talk to him."

"Speak to him in Romansh."

Luca nodded. They entered the boy's inner sanctum that contained a desk and chair. He noticed the slender, dark-haired boy lying on the bed fully clothed in shorts and a T-shirt. He was turned toward the wall away from them, minus a lower leg.

His mother brought in a chair from the kitchen. "Bless you for coming," she whispered. "I'll be in the kitchen if you need me."

Luca pulled the desk chair around so they could both sit near the bed.

Bella spoke first. "Hasper? My name is Bella. You remind me of myself. When I was sixteen and went skiing, I did something I was forbidden to do. A big sign warned of avalanche danger, but I didn't care so I started down the trail.

"A very brave eighteen-year-old guy chased after me to stop me. But I didn't listen to him because I was showing off in front of him. Suddenly there was an avalanche. It came crashing down and could have killed us. Later at the hospital I woke up just fine, but my mother told me the other guy would probably lose his leg. Worse, he was no longer at the hospital and I couldn't contact him."

If Hasper was listening, Luca couldn't tell, but hearing the emotion in Bella brought his old feelings of pain and despair to the surface.

"His name was Luca Torriani, the guy who'd been put on the Swiss ski training team for the Olympics. But he'd never be able to be an Olympian now because of me. His story was on the news and in all the papers."

To Luca's shock, the boy slowly sat up and turned around to look. He stared at her, then at Luca. A connection had been made.

"For years I wanted to die, Hasper, because I never did find out what happened to his leg. I'd lie in bed every night and sob over the terrible thing I'd done, until ten years later I saw him again. The man right here with me *is* Luca Torriani. He had to undergo an operation on his leg, but it changed his life for the better. Show him, Luca."

He pulled up his pant leg so the boy could see the scars. Bella was seeing them for the first time too. "I've got screws in there holding my leg together, Hasper. I don't ski competitively anymore, but thanks to the doctor, I can walk and move around like any other person."

Bella leaned forward. "You have no idea how happy I am that he can walk when I thought he'd lost his leg because of me. I realize you've lost your lower leg because your father told you never to drive the tractor. But you can be given an artificial one and—"

"And it won't require screws," Luca took over. "You'll be able to walk around just like your buddies. You can hike and do whatever you want. In long pants no one will ever know. When you're old enough, you'll be able to drive a tractor if that's what you want to do to help your mom."

"Hasper?" Bella joined in. "Your father wouldn't want you to lie around on this bed until you die. Neither does your mom. Pretty soon you'll get sick of it the way I did because that's what I used to do. Do you understand?"

The boy nodded.

"Your parents don't want you to feel bad. Your father is up in heaven proud of you for trying to help her. So there was a tractor accident. Accidents happen to everyone. All you have to do is get fitted for a new leg and you'll be better than ever. Show all your friends you're tough."

Luca moved to the side of the bed. "I'm

a doctor, and I'll help you. Will you let me examine your leg?"

It took a minute before he said, "Okay."

The boy lay back down while Luca looked him over. He was satisfied there was enough soft tissue to cushion the remaining bone. The knee joint was intact and the skin on his limb was in good condition.

"You're a perfect candidate for a prosthetic leg and will have a lot of mobility."

"What does that thing look like?"

Thrilled they were getting through to him, Luca smiled. "A lot better than my leg. When you go to the hospital with your mom, the prosthetist will show you everything. I can tell you this much. The socket is the mold of your limb and fits over it. The suspension system is how it stays attached. It won't hurt."

"Will you be there?"

Luca and Bella exchanged glances. "We'll both be there all the way."

They could hear his mind working before he said, "I'll try it."

Bella got to her feet. "I'll go get your mom. She'll want to hear this wonderful news!"

More rejoicing ensued. Hasper's mother would make an appointment for the fitting and let Luca know when it could be done.

A half hour later, after more tears and hugs, they left the Bazzell home and drove to the hospital where the helicopter sat.

"A miracle has happened, Bella. It's all due to you. Today I relived our past and am in awe over your desire to help the unfortunate of this world. One day that boy will praise your name."

Her fantastic violet eyes looked into his. "The praise goes to the man who gave no thought to himself when he skied down that mountain to save me. I can't find the right words to tell you how...how grateful I am." Her stammer covered something else she would have said that gave him hope.

They traveled back to the town in their rental car, but en route she received a phone call from her brother. When she picked up, she turned on the speaker. "Vincenzo?"

"Thank goodness you answered. Where are you?"

"In Glarus with Luca. We've just been to the Bazzell farm so Luca could examine the boy Hasper for a prosthetic leg."

"Wow. That's fantastic. I wish I didn't have worrisome news."

"What's wrong?"

"It's Nonna. She's taken another turn for the worse. I think you'd better see her before it's too late."

Bella nodded. "I couldn't agree more. Let Mamma know I'll head straight to Innsbruck in the helicopter now. From there I'll fly to Sardinia."

"I wish I could be with you—"

"I'll go with her," Luca broke in. "I only wish there was something I could do to help. I like your *nonna*."

"Nonna thought the world of you too, buddy."

When they hung up, he stared at Bella. "Is it all right if I come with you? Tell me now if it isn't, and I'll arrange my journey back to Scuol."

"No, no. I remember how much she liked you. I think it will make her happy."

Little by little Luca felt that maybe he'd one day win his heart's desire.

The flight ended at five in the afternoon in Cagliari, the capital city of over one hundred and fifty thousand people. Many times Bella and Vincenzo had hiked to the hilltop *castello* during their visits and had explored the ancient walled old town overlooking the vista below.

Bella's grandmother had been put in a suite reserved for the Cusso royal family. The attending physician greeted her with enthusiasm. She introduced Luca as Dr. Torriani. "How is my *nonna*?"

"Princess Caderina is coming along from the latest bout of pneumonia, Princess Baldasseri." Bella moaned inwardly at the royal appellation. Certain things would never change. "If she continues to do well, I'll let her go home. It will do her good to see her granddaughter. Go right in. She hasn't had much of an appetite, but I know your visit will do her good."

"Thank you."

Luca followed her into the hospital room. She walked over to the bed where her grandmother lay with her head slightly elevated. She'd been hooked up with oxygen. Her hair had turned white when it had once been red like the red hair Bella's mother had inherited. The two women had the same bone structure and had both been reputed beauties.

"Nonna?"

All Bella had to do was say the word and her grandmother's eyelids opened. "Bella, Bella—" she cried and tried to sit up.

"I came as soon as I could." Bella leaned over and kissed both her cheeks. "It's so wonderful to see you and I miss you so much. I'm sorry you've been suffering."

"I'm all right now that you're here. Bring the chairs around and sit so we can talk." Luca did her bidding. When they were seated, she studied him. "I'm a little worried, Bella. Am I seeing things or is it possible the man smiling down at me is Luca Torriani?"

"You're not wrong, Princess Caderina," he interjected.

"You've grown into an impossibly handsome man."

"He's a sports medicine doctor too."

Her grandmother knew everything, but she pretended otherwise. "Luca? I was crazy about you the first time I met you with Vincenzo and Bella. It was clear that my *bimba* was besotted with you all those years you were growing up."

"We both had it pretty bad back then." Luca laughed.

"And now?"

"We're just friends," Luca interjected again before Bella could say anything.

"Yes," Bella blurted. "He's helped with one of my charity cases. A little boy who needs a prosthetic leg."

"God's work. How wonderful! Come give me a kiss, Luca."

Bella watched through tears as her beloved grandmother and Luca embraced.

"*Bimba?* Did I ever tell you how much your mother loved your father? Before they married, he became so ill from the flu he almost died. She vowed to become a nun rather than marry anyone else if anything happened to him. I believed her at the time and still believe she would have."

"I didn't know that about Papa or her." Bella was shocked over the revelation.

"When he recovered, I'm sure she never wanted to think or talk about it again. But now I want to know about you and Luca.

What's going on with your lives? Tell me everything. Leave nothing out."

Her love warmed Bella's heart. She and Luca leaned closer and they told her about their separate lives. They talked together until after ten when her grandmother finally closed her eyes and fell asleep. The hospital arranged for her and Luca to stay in the suite on cots so they could be near her. They set up their beds close together in the other room.

Luca propped himself on one elbow. "Your grandmother is a wonder, Bella."

"I know. No one has a kinder heart."

"She's like my mother," Luca confessed.

"I can't believe I've never met her."

"Maybe one day." He could pray for that.

"I'm just thankful Nonna is rallying from this latest attack. I can leave tomorrow knowing she's all right for now."

Bella lay back on the pillow and slept all night facing the man she hungered for in secret. The next morning, they ate breakfast with her grandmother. When Bella leaned over to give her a kiss, her grandmother grasped her arm. "Don't worry," she whispered. "Everything is going to work out for you and Luca."

"I don't know."

"Yes, you do. Don't keep him waiting too long. A man like Luca only comes along once in a thousand years."

That was exactly what Bella thought too. "God bless you, Nonna. I'll visit again very soon."

Luca gave her grandmother another hug before they left the hospital for the airport. On the flight back to Innsbruck they talked about the revelation learned the night before.

"Nonna confirmed something for me I've always known, Luca. My father would have done anything for Mother. What I don't understand is why Mother never told me or Vincenzo that he almost died, or that she threatened to become a nun if he didn't make it."

"I think I do. If you don't know what she went through, you can't use it for leverage against her."

She turned to him. "I'm surprised you're not a psychiatrist."

"I did rounds in psychiatry before choosing sports medicine."

"And did it give you any insight into why your father has no use for royals? There has to be a reason."

"Lately, I've been wondering the same thing. The next time I talk to my mother, I intend to ask her what secret she has held back that she hasn't told me about." They smiled at each other in mutual understanding before she turned away. Another second and she'd tell him she couldn't live without him.

Upon landing in Innsbruck, they boarded the helicopter and flew back to the palace in Scuol. They got in his car and he drove her to her apartment.

"I'm glad you came with me, Luca," she said in a trembling voice before getting out.

"So am I. It meant everything for the three of us to be together like old times."

Old times…

She rushed inside the apartment before he could see the tears streaming down her face. Before she got in bed, she phoned her mother.

"Bella? Where are you?" she asked in a strident voice.

"In bed in my room. Nonna was doing so well, I was able to leave this morning."

"We both know you were with Luca Torriani."

"Yes. Nonna remembered him and it made her happy to see him."

Her mother made a strange sound in her throat. "She's not in her right mind."

There was no point in arguing. "The doctor will send her back to the palace with her caregiver tomorrow. I'm so thankful, and I believe this crisis has been averted."

"But not the one you continue to create. When will you move back home and stop this nonsense?" she demanded.

"I'm in my new home."

"You've been neglecting your grandparents and Prince Antonio."

Bella gripped the phone tighter. "I've been doing important charity work. I'll be over the day after tomorrow and spend time with all of you."

"You're not in your right mind either."

The divine right of kings Luca had once referred to about his father came to mind.

Bella drew in a deep breath. "In that case I'll become a nun, the way you would have done if Papa hadn't survived the flu before your marriage. *Buona notte*, Mamma. Never forget that I really do love you."

The next evening at the condo, Luca phoned Bella.

"Are you alone?" he asked, barely able to keep the jealousy from his voice.

"You don't have the right to ask me that, Luca," she sighed.

"You're right, and I'm not going to beat about the bush. I can't go on like this. I told your grandmother that we were just friends, but the truth is that can never be true. You're the love of my life, Bella. Being with you on the campout, and in Sardinia, has made me hungry for all the things I've missed in the years we've been apart. I can help you with your charity work from a distance, but I can't be around you if I can't be with you. I love you. That's it. I don't want to play cat and mouse anymore. It hurts too much. Next Saturday after work I'll be meeting with some colleagues at the Wine Cellar for drinks. If you'd like to meet me there at seven for dinner, I'll look for you. In case you don't come, I'll know you've moved on with Prince Antonio, or another one, for good." On that note he hung up.

After what seemed like a month of torture, Saturday night arrived. Luca said good-night to his colleagues in the lounge of the Wine Cellar and waited for Bella to arrive. It was five to seven. He'd give her fifteen minutes. If she didn't show, he'd know everything was over.

When the clock said twenty after seven, he left the restaurant. Devastated that it really was over with her, he hurried down the narrow, outside stone staircase. Halfway to the ground he collided with a woman rushing up the stairs.

"Luca!" She clung to him. "Thank heaven I didn't miss you! My car has a flat tire and I had to call a taxi." Her voice shook.

When he could gather his wits, he realized he was holding the old Bella in his arms. "You should have phoned me. I would have picked you up."

"The important thing is that I'm here now. I love being independent, but the truth is, I hate this life without you. You're the man I've always loved and I don't want to lose you."

"But Prince Antonio…"

"I explained everything to Tonio that night you saw him at my apartment. Whatever was going to happen between you and I, or wasn't, he deserved the truth. And the truth is that there is no one else but you for me. There never has been. Tonio is a wonderful man and he'll make some lucky woman very happy someday. I wanted him to be free to find that as soon as possible."

Luca's elation knew no bounds, but people needed to get past them. "Come on. Let's go inside and talk about everything over dinner." He cupped her elbow and they climbed the rest of the staircase.

Her lips brushed his jaw as they made their way inside the four-hundred-year-old restaurant. "Do you know I've never been here?"

"We both know why," he murmured. "Princess Bella wasn't allowed to dine in local establishments with locals like me. Thank heaven there will be no more of that."

The host recognized her immediately, but when Luca shook his head slightly, the other man remained silent. *"Vogliamo mangiare fuori."*

"Si, signor."

At Luca's request they were led to the patio. No diners sat out there yet. The air had warmed up since morning. Luca welcomed the mild temperature and knew Bella would enjoy the surrounding plants and flowers. After he helped seat her, a waiter came to bring them menus. They made their choices, then Luca examined the wine list.

"We'd like champagne first. Krug, I believe. Make it Clos du Mesnil."

"Subito, signor."

Luca smiled at the breathtaking woman seated across from him. "You've never looked more beautiful."

"If I said the same thing to you, I know you wouldn't like it."

"Try me."

"Oh, Luca." Above flushed cheeks, her eyes radiated purple. "I love you so much. I want to believe we will always be together, just like this."

"You do?" He reached in his trouser pocket and brought out the ring.

She stared at it in disbelief. "You still have it with you?"

"I never gave up on you, but are you sure you're ready for the next step?" he teased.

"I want it so much, I'm dying."

"Well, we can't have that." He reached for her left hand and slid it home on her ring finger.

At that moment the waiter came with the champagne and filled their glasses. Luca held on to her and lifted his glass with his left hand. "To the only woman in the world for me. *Ti amo, il mio tesoro.*"

She raised her glass. *"Ti adoro,* Luca. *Mio eroe."* She squeezed his hand hard. "My dreams began with you. No other man could make them a reality." He touched her glass and they began drinking the delicious champagne. "Shall we ask Father Viret to marry us?"

"Not if your mother hears about it, and she will."

"It doesn't matter."

"Even so, I have a better idea. Tomorrow is Sunday. We could request a meeting with Father Denis at the church. He was our family priest when we lived here. I imagine he'll be delighted to perform the ceremony."

While they smiled into each other's eyes, the waiter brought their salmon. Luca had also ordered *capuns* and *maluns*.

They both were starving and ate everything. "This food is marvelous, Luca. I love these crumbly potatoes and this sausage ball wrapped in chard."

"These are my favorite dishes."

"That's something about you I didn't know. I'll have to ask your mother for the recipes so I can cook them for you."

"We'll invite them to the condo and she'll show you. Nothing will thrill her more."

"Or me. Growing up I knew how much you loved her, and I always wanted to meet her." She finished her salmon. "Do you think your father will come with her once we're man and wife?" He heard a little tremor in her voice.

"We can hope his heart will soften one day. As for your mother, we'll just have to take it a step at a time. Maybe when our first baby is born."

She chuckled. "I love your optimism."

"Vuoi il dolce?" The waiter had just come to their table.

"Do you want dessert, Bella?"

"I couldn't. The champagne was all I needed."

Luca thanked him and asked for the bill. He put some money on the table.

"Let's go. Before I take you to your apartment and look at your car, I want to stop at the condo. It's going to be our home."

They left the restaurant. He helped her down the outside stairs and they headed to his car. Before long they'd wound their way back to his condo. After he walked her in the living room, he pulled her down on the couch. She lifted her eyes to him. "For us to be alone like this feels too good to be true."

"You took the words right out of my mouth, and I'm afraid it presents a problem."

She sat straighter. "What do you mean?"

"I have one rule. I want to be married to the woman I love when I take her to bed for the first time. Can you understand that?" he whispered.

Bella laid a hand against his jaw. "Yes, because I know you. Over the years you've proven to be the most honorable man alive. No wonder you left the tent on our campout."

"I've already made inquiries about getting married. I'm hoping we can find a way to make it as quick a process as possible."

"I hope so too. Perhaps being a princess will come in useful for something. I don't want to wait another moment to be your wife."

"Thank heaven for you, Bella." Luca's dark head descended and he kissed the life out of her before getting to his feet. "Come on. I'll run you home and change your tire. Tomorrow morning I'll come by for you at nine. We'll go to the church first, then I'll take you out for lunch and we'll make plans."

A half hour later, he walked her to her door. "Try to get some sleep."

She threw her arms around his neck. "I'll be waiting for you in the morning." Her tears started. "Thank you for being wonderful you. I'm the most blessed woman in the world to be engaged to you. When you drive away, I'm going to worry about you until I see you tomorrow. I'd die if anything happened to you."

"Don't say that. I promise we're going to have a perfect life together. *Buona notte, sposa mia.*" In his mind she already was his wife.

She gave him a final kiss that lit him on fire. After he got in his car, she waved. The sight of Bella standing there filled him with a jubilance he'd never experienced before.

He was still walking on air when he entered his condo. He showered and got in bed. For the next hour he answered half a dozen phone messages from his service. There was another message, this one from his father. It didn't require an answer.

I've heard about you joining the Lemond Institute. You've made the biggest mistake of your life. Consider yourself warned.

CHAPTER EIGHT

BELLA WANDERED AROUND the apartment, still having trouble believing that she and Luca were really, finally together. Once she'd showered and washed her hair, she got in bed and lay there for a long time dreaming of the wedding night to come. It felt like she'd been waiting forever to be alone with Luca and love him in every sense of the word.

On Sunday morning she got up and put on a navy print dress appropriate to wear to the church. She left her hair long and slipped on heeled sandals.

At five to nine she reached for her purse and walked out in front of the apartment to wait for him. The sky had few clouds and she noticed the air was much warmer. What a wonderful day!

At five after nine Luca pulled in the parking area. He jumped out of the car and hurried over to her. "You look fabulous."

"So do you." He'd dressed in a gray suit and tie. No man could compare to him.

His eyes played over her face and hair. "I can't fathom that you're going to be mine." He cupped her face and kissed her with a growing hunger. "How did you sleep?"

"I think you know the answer to that."

Luca chuckled and helped her into the car. "Tomorrow we both have to go to work and do our jobs. All I want to do today is make the most of it with you." He started the engine and they drove out to the main road. "Once we've talked to Father Denis, we can do whatever you'd like."

"I don't dare tell you what I'd rather do than anything else because I'm committed to your plan. I *can* wait until we're man and wife."

He gripped her hand as they made their way to the eighteenth-century church. The entrance to the office lay around the side. Once he'd parked, Bella jumped out and walked inside with him, eager to talk to the priest.

"Princess Baldasseri—" the receptionist

exclaimed in surprise when she saw Bella enter the office with Luca. She got to her feet and bowed.

"Buongiorno, signora."

Luca walked over to her desk. "I'm Dr. Torriani and have made an appointment with Father Denis. Will you please let him know we're here?"

"I'm so sorry, but he was called away. He left word that any requests regarding you and Princess Baldasseri must go through Father Viret first."

So…the war had started. "I'm sorry too. He was my priest in my youth."

"He said as much. Would you like me to ring Father Viret?"

"That won't be necessary."

Luca exchanged a glance with Bella before he thanked the church receptionist and cupped Bella's elbow to leave. He continued escorting her back outside and helped her in the car. "I should never have underestimated them," he muttered.

"Who?"

Luca pulled out his cell and found the text. "This came from my father last night.

I was going to show it to you while we ate, but you need to see it now."

When Bella read it, she groaned. "The team is at it again."

"Yes, they are, so let's pick a time to meet at the civic center tomorrow to apply for our marriage license. Then we'll find a local magistrate to marry us. I can get away from the office for a short time."

"We'll have to go first thing in the morning, Luca. I'm due in Chur on charity business at noon tomorrow and will be gone until Friday with more meetings in nearby towns." She put a hand on his arm. "Why don't we go home and change? I feel like a trip to the mountains."

"You're reading my mind." He winked at her before starting the engine. "We'll pick up food at the deli on the way."

"Even though I'm no longer a princess, it appears we're going to keep my security busy."

He grinned. "It's good for them."

"You know they're spying on us. I wonder if my mother pays them extra."

"I doubt it."

They drove back to her apartment. While

she changed into jeans and a dark green pullover, she received a text on her cell.

Please come home, Bella, so we can talk about the situation. You've hurt Prince Antonio. How can you live with this man in Vincenzo's condo and forget you're a princess?

Bella shook her head. There was no situation, only the one with her mother, who knew nothing, thought the worst and created a nightmare by insisting Bella live her life as a royal.

After pocketing her phone, Bella put on her hiking boots and went into the kitchen. Luca was filling their water bottles. Once that was done, he drove them to his condo, where he changed into a dark brown turtleneck and jeans.

The man looked so gorgeous, she wanted them to go into his bedroom and never come out. Instead, she wrapped her arms around his waist from behind. "I feel like we're playing house."

"We *are* playing, and we need to keep playing until we say 'I do.' A man can only take so much."

"Why does a man always say that when in truth, a *woman* can only take so much too. Believe me."

"Bella..." He turned around and gave her a kiss to die for.

Breathless, she pulled away first. "We'd better go now while I can still honor your rule."

They left the condo and drove through town to the deli. "I'll run inside. What sounds good, *bellissima*?"

"Pasta? Salad? Whatever appeals to you."

"I'll bring a couple of colas too."

"Perfect. You're perfect." She kissed the side of his hard jaw.

Sometime later they found an ideal spot a little way up the mountain with a grassy slope ideal for a picnic. He locked up the car and they hiked until noon. She worried he had to be starving by now and suggested they go back to their spot to eat.

While she carried the blanket from his trunk and spread it out, Luca brought their food and drinks from the cooler.

"This is heaven, Bella *mia*." They'd both stretched out half raised on their sides to face each other while they ate. His expression grew thoughtful. "I heard at least half a dozen dings on your phone while we were hiking, yet you didn't answer. Why?"

"After what happened to us at the church, I knew these messages were from my mother. She sent the first one while I was changing for our hike. I didn't respond."

"What did she say?"

Bella pulled out her cell and let him read the text. "I was going to show this to you." They had no secrets from each other. "She assumes we're already living together in the biblical sense."

His penetrating eyes focused on her. "Only you and I know the truth. Your poor mother cares about your princess status deep in her psyche. Don't tell me this message doesn't bring you pain. I know differently."

She let out a sigh. "It all depends on your definition of pain, Luca. Yes, it pains me to disappoint her because she has loved being a princess. She wants that life for me. It has been her experience and I'm happy for her. But I'm my own person and never liked being Princess Bella. To continue any longer would mean living a complete lie. That's a pain I refuse to abide and you know the truth of that in your inner core."

"I believe you," Luca murmured. "You've just described life with my father. He's tried to turn me into a clone of himself. You don't have to be born a royal to have a fixation about your ambitions for your children. I don't want to disappoint him. He's a good man. Successful. But like you, I'm my own person and have hated living a lie that I feared would put me in an early grave."

Her eyes filled with tears. "Then we're in this no matter what."

"*No matter what.* It's one thing for them to have prevented us from being together ten years ago when they could see how we felt about each other. But we're adults now and this time they won't prevail."

He moved everything so he could gather her in his arms. The sun poured down on them while they gave in to their longing. Bella had forgotten everything in the ecstasy of his kisses when she heard a whistle. They stopped long enough to find out where it came from. Four teenage guys were out hiking and waved to them. The little monkeys.

She chuckled before Luca waved back and started kissing her again. She was dying to be closer to him. "I wish we could be put in a coma until our wedding day."

He kissed her throat, sending delicious chills through her body. "Don't think I haven't thought of it."

"Being out here with you is heaven."

"Except there's a forest service ranger coming up the road. I think we've provided enough entertainment for today. Let's leave and I'll drive you to see my new place of work."

She let out an excited cry and sat up once more. "Have you decorated it?"

"Not yet."

"Then let's stop at the condo for your things. I'll help put up your diplomas. I want to inspect the office where my future husband will be spending his days while we're apart."

"It won't be that different from my office in Saint Moritz."

"Oh, yes, it will, unless Adele has been hired too." Both of them chuckled as they carried everything back to the car and headed for Scuol. "When word gets around that the famous, most attractive, drop-dead fabulous Dr. Torriani is there, he'll be deluged with admirers. It's a good thing you're getting married soon. I think I'll put a big picture of myself on your desk as an instant reminder that you're *taken*!"

Rich laughter rumbled out of him, a sound she could listen to forever.

Within an hour Bella learned that the Lemond Institute of doctors took up a portion of a building near the hospital. Luca had been given an office on the second floor. They carried two boxes from the car and got busy deciding where to put everything.

While she was hanging the last diploma on the wall, Luca went out to the car to bring in some extra cable cord for his computer. Suddenly she heard a knock and turned around.

Two men stood in the doorway. One had blond hair. The older one had dark hair with silver at the temples. Bella recognized him immediately from Luca's pictures at the condo, but she'd never met him. His nice-looking, distinguished father hadn't wasted a moment. She wondered if Luca knew he'd come.

The blond man smiled. *"Buon pomeriggio, signorina.* I don't believe we've met. I'm Dr. Raspar." She knew he had to recognize her, but he didn't act on it. "This is Dr. Jaronas Torriani. He's looking for his son."

"I'm Alectrona Cusso." On their hike they'd decided she would use that name around everyone. After their marriage, she'd be Signora Torriani. *"Che piacere incontrarla."* Except that she wasn't that happy to meet them at the moment. "Luca will be right back. As you can see, we're setting up his office."

Dr. Raspar grinned. "Luca didn't tell me you were coming in today."

"I'm not surprised. We only celebrated our engagement last night."

His father stood there frozen in place. Whether he liked it or not—and he didn't— she and Luca were in, *no matter what.*

"That sly dog. All the unmarried women in this building will be crushed when they find out. May I offer my congratulations. We're thrilled to have Scuol's famous young ski legend and soon-to-be wife join our staff at last."

The innocent comment was a reminder that would always cause her pain. "He's thrilled too, believe me. So am I."

"Well, I'll leave you here with your future daughter-in-law, Dr. Torriani." His gaze flicked to Bella. "I'm sure I'll be seeing you again soon. We're planning a dinner to welcome Luca and at the Hotel Belaval next Saturday evening and will want you to join us, Signorina Cusso."

"I can't wait, Dr. Raspar. Thank you."

When he disappeared, Luca's father moved inside the office staring daggers at her.

"We finally meet in person," Bella spoke first. "I've always loved your son and am humbled that he wants to marry me."

His brows furrowed. "You still have the power to let him go before it's too late, Princess Baldasseri." His voice possessed a deep timbre like Luca's.

Just then Luca unexpectedly walked in on them holding a loop of cord. "It was too late the first time I met Bella."

His father turned to him. "You can't marry

in the church. If you marry outside the church, it won't be a true marriage."

"It will be to God and to us." Luca walked around to hook up the cable to his computer. "That's what thousands and thousands of couples believe who are united in a civil marriage."

"I'm talking about you, Luca, and the way you were raised. You could marry any woman."

"I'm planning to marry the only woman I want forever, Papa. Bella was only eight years old when I met her. She was holding Vincenzo's injured dog Rex. When I told her we didn't have a dog, she said I could come over any time and play with him. She had a sweetness and genuine charm that captured my heart instantly. No other woman has ever come close."

"I felt the same way about you," Bella said in a trembling voice.

The conversation between father and son was no different from Bella's conversation with her mother. Right now she felt compelled to defend Luca. "We've already tried to plan for a private church marriage, Dr.

Torriani. It's up to you and my mother to allow that to happen."

"No, it's up to you, Princess Baldasseri. You have the power to let him go, otherwise you will divide the entire Torriani family forever. Do the godly thing and give up this foolishness. Do you deliberately want to estrange Luca from me and his mother?" His cheeks grew ruddy. "If Prince Baldasseri were alive—"

"Bella's father is no longer with us," Luca broke in. "But if he were, it would make no difference." He walked toward her and put his arm around her shoulders.

"Trying to guilt Bella into getting your own way won't do any good, Papa. Her mother has her own strong feelings just as you do. Bella, who's no longer a princess, and I have our own strong feelings too and Mamma has given us her blessing. Any estrangement you've caused is with my mother and no one else. Let that be the end of it so we can all get along."

"Get along—" His father ground his voice to a thunderous pitch. "You truly have lost your mind."

Luca hugged her closer. "When Bella

and I have children, you'll be their *nonno* and *nonna*. I know how much you long for grandchildren one day. Think about the future before you say anything else, Papa. You have the power to mend this estrangement that should never *ever* had happened."

"There'll be no royals in the Torriani family tree," his father pronounced like an edict. "I'll see to that." He wheeled around and left the office in a fury.

Bella eyed the love of her life, aching for him because of this impasse. "He's thrown down the gauntlet under no uncertain terms."

"My father did that ten years ago."

She brushed her lips against his chin. "I met Dr. Raspar."

"I know. We saw each other as he was coming out of the building." Those lightning green eyes flashed between black lashes. "I asked him to avoid calling you Princess. He's still in shock over meeting you in person."

"He was very charming and mentioned getting together for a dinner next Saturday."

"You don't know what it will mean to

have my fiancée there at my side. I'll be the envy of every man in sight."

"That's how it was when I was around you at school years ago. The girls hated me for having an in with the school's hero through my brother."

He shook his head and kissed her. "You didn't need an in. We were lucky he provided such great cover for both of us."

She kissed him back.

"Let's grab a bite to eat and get you home, Bella. We've both got a big week to get through. I know you have to leave for Chur. How would you feel about us going to the civic center first thing in the morning to nail down our wedding ceremony? It opens at eight thirty. I'd like to be there on the dot and get things settled. Otherwise, I don't think I'll be able to function."

"That makes two of us."

They left his office for the car. Darkness had fallen. On the way to her apartment, they stopped at a drive-through for takeout. A half hour later they were eating their dinner at her kitchen counter when Luca's phone rang. He glanced at the caller ID. "It's your brother."

She put down the last of her *croque-monsieur* and got up to stand next to him. "When you answer it, will you put it on speaker?"

Luca nodded. "I believe you're as curious as I am." He clicked on and pressed the button so they could both hear him. "What's up, Vincenzo? Bella is right here with me."

"Thank heaven. Now you both need to hear this. I've been at the palace to see Mamma and the grandparents. As I was leaving to go back to Zernez, I discovered your father has come there to see her. I hung around to find out what was going on. They're prepared to do whatever it takes to stop you two from getting married."

"We found that out at the church today," Luca muttered. Bella put a hand on his shoulder.

"Mamma has also put pressure on the regional chief magistrate to prevent a civil marriage."

Upon hearing that news, Luca's gaze fused with Bella's. "Thanks for the heads-up, Vincenzo. We'll do something else, even if we have to leave Switzerland."

"Let's not go that far. I'll think of something, but there's more I have to tell you. Bella?"

"I'm listening."

"According to Mamma, Nonna Caderina has grown worse again. Our mother wants you to fly to Sardinia with her and stay with her for a while. She plans to leave tomorrow. I'm sure you'll be getting a call from her in a few minutes."

Bella squeezed Luca's shoulder. "She was getting better when we left her. Do you believe she's suddenly a lot worse?"

"I don't know. I find the timing suspicious because of your plans with Luca, but you never know."

"Of course not. I love Nonna so much."

"Don't we all. Since I'm still at the palace, I'm going back upstairs to tell her I'm going to Sardinia with her. I need to find out exactly what's going on. Francesca can't take off any more work so I'll be coming right back and report."

"I'm sorry you have to leave your wife."

"So am I, but I know she has you and Luca to lean on."

"Absolutely! We're crazy about her."

"She feels the same way about you two.

I'll stay in close touch. Luca? Hang in there."

"Always." Luca had already gotten to his feet and put his arm around Bella. "We'll be waiting for your call. Come home safely."

He clicked off and pulled her against him, burying his face in her hair.

"My poor brother," she moaned the words.

Luca kissed her temple. "Maybe you should go again so you can see your grandmother and satisfy your worry."

She looked up at him. "I can't go yet since I'm leaving for Chur by helicopter tomorrow. I'll be gone until Friday and meeting with various people in other towns. But after I return, I won't plan anything else until after we're married."

"What if it's a true emergency?"

"Then I'll drop everything to be with her."

"In that case we'll go together."

"Do you have any idea how you've transformed my world? How much I'm going to miss you this week?"

"Tell me about it, *mia principessa*. I need to leave now or I'm in danger of breaking my promise."

She followed him to the door. "Take care, Luca. Life would mean nothing without you now."

"You're the one I worry about. Fly back to me, Bella. We'll talk on the phone this evening."

"I'm living for it." But one more breathtaking kiss from him would never be enough.

The week without Bella yawned wide for Luca. Vincenzo stayed in touch with him. On Wednesday evening he came by the condo. The two men hugged and sat down to eat some muesli cereal with milk, their favorite snack in the palace kitchen when they were young.

"I'll give you the bad news first. Our grandmother Caderina has pneumonia and it's growing worse."

"I'm not surprised." Luca finished his coffee. "What's the good news?"

Vincenzo sat back in the chair with a smile. "I've done some favors for Father Jaines in Zernez. He will be able to marry you up on the mountain. Francesca and I will bring him. All you have to do is be there with my sister."

"How can I ever thank you."

"You don't need to. You're my best friend, I'm happy to do it." He got up from the table. "I'm sorry for everything my mother has done to keep you two apart."

The second he left the condo, Luca called the love of his life. "Bella? Your brother just left. I'm afraid your grandmother is going downhill."

"I can believe it."

"He also gave us some good news. We're getting married by Father Jaines from Zernez, who will marry us up on the mountain. He and Francesca will bring him."

"You mean to our own Garden of Eden?"

"Where else? Rest assured your brother and Francesca will be our witnesses. Maybe the mountain hares will join us too."

"How did he accomplish that?"

"He did the priest a few favors."

"So, royals do have their uses once in a while." He smiled. "Your father would be scandalized."

"My mother will be delirious with joy."

Bella's cry of delight caused him to hold his phone away for a second. "I take it you're happy."

This time laughter bubbled out of her. "I'm in heaven."

"So am I."

"*Ti amo*, Luca."

"*Sei tutto per me*, Bella." She really was his everything. "I'll be waiting for you at your apartment on Friday night." He hung up and went to the kitchen for more coffee. The next order of business was to call Signora Bazzell. He needed to hear details about plans for her son.

CHAPTER NINE

FRIDAY AFTERNOON BELLA arrived in the helicopter behind the palace. Before driving to the apartment to meet Luca, she went inside to see her mother. The family were eating in the dining room. Bella walked around to give each of them a kiss.

"At last! Sit down and have dinner with us," her mother demanded.

"I can't, Mamma. I have other plans, but I just wanted to tell you I'll be flying to Cagliari again soon so I can spend a longer time with Nonna."

"Don't you dare fly there this time with Luca Torriani."

Bella took a quick breath. "He's my fiancé. We're going to be married."

"Oh, no, you're not! When will you be home again?" she demanded. "You've been neglecting your grandparents."

"I've been doing important charity work. I'll be over the day after tomorrow and spend time with all of you. Until after Luca and I are married, I won't make any more commitments to the charity."

"You're not in your right mind either. There will be no marriage."

Taking a deep breath, she said, "Love you all." Bella blew them a kiss and left the palace, driving over speed. Only one thing, one person, was on her mind.

"Luca?" she cried when she saw him waiting for her.

He caught her in his arms and they entered the apartment. *"Mia principessa!"* After swinging her around, he carried her to the couch where they tried to make up for nearly a week's deprivation. Half lying on him, no kiss could satisfy their deep hunger for each other.

She covered his face with kisses, pouring out her love. "I never want to be away from you this long again." Upset after seeing her mother, tears came to her eyes, causing Luca to lift his head.

"What's wrong, Bella?"

"I went inside the palace to see the family after I flew in. Mother is impossible."

"I expected as much." He kissed her hungrily. "Like my father, nothing she says or does is a surprise."

"But under the circumstances it still amazes me how totally inflexible they both are."

"Forget them." Luca caught her wet face in his hands and kissed her again. "Guess what? Hasper's mother has asked us to meet her at the Glarus hospital tomorrow at noon for his operation."

"Nothing could please me more than to hear her son is willing to go through the procedure."

"It's the best news." After a pause, "Now I have something else you need to know."

"What's happened?"

"Mamma phoned me on my way to work because my father was with a patient and couldn't hear her. Yesterday on the phone I told her I knew a secret about your mother and would tell her later. Then I kiddingly asked her what secret she knew about my father's dislike of royalty. I didn't expect an answer. This morning to my amazement, she told me something that explains so much, I hardly know where to begin."

Her heart began to thud. "Has she known this secret a long time?"

"Yes, but my father doesn't realize she knows anything."

Bella swallowed hard. "Am I going to like it or hate it?"

"Hate."

She cringed. "Please don't keep me in suspense—"

"Did I ever tell you about my great-grandfather Basil Torriani?"

"No."

"I never knew anything about him except that he was a tailor. But that's only a portion of his whole life story. It seems he was born and lived in Innsbruck, Austria. He attended medical school there."

"He was a doctor?"

"A well-known one," Luca informed her. "His career in ophthalmology led him to take care of your great-aunt Elsa Baldasseri in San Vitano."

"You're kidding!"

"There's something else you're not going

to believe. She went blind after he operated on her eyes." Bella gasped.

"The King, Filipo Baldasseri, your great-great-grandfather, blamed him for causing his daughter's blindness. According to his *mamma*, who'd heard stories from her mother-in-law, he couldn't have saved her sight. In fact, he'd tried with all his might to restore it. But the King accused him and let it be known publicly. It ended his medical career and a humiliated Basil left Innsbruck in disgrace."

A groan escaped Bella's throat.

"It's no wonder my father became an allergist and didn't want me to be a surgeon."

"What a tragedy, Luca."

"Imagine having to give up his practice. He settled in Lucerne, Switzerland, with his family, where he worked in a tailor's shop until he died. It was his son, my grandfather Rudolfo Torriani, a doctor, who eventually settled in Scuol. His wife was born here and she wanted to be near her family. The Torriani family never forgave the King or anyone with the name Baldasseri."

"I don't blame them!" Bella cried. "How absolutely ghastly. No wonder your father holds such hate for me. It's a miracle he joined with Mother to fight you and me. Is there no way to prove that Basil wasn't responsible so his name can be cleared in a public way?"

"I don't know yet. The problem is, my mother learned about this years ago. She's afraid to cause any trouble, but she wanted me to know the truth because she loves us both."

"I love her more than ever."

"I feel the same way about you. Tomorrow I'll pick you up at eight and we'll drive to the hospital to take the helicopter. Let's pray it all goes well with Hasper." He eased away from her with reluctance and got to his feet.

She followed him. "How did I live this long without you?"

"I've asked that question about you thousands of times, but we're back together now and nothing will ever separate us again."

Those words rang in her ears throughout the night. The next morning she shivered in the cool air as they drove to the hospital to board the helicopter. Once strapped inside he grasped her hand. "We're a normal couple now. How does it feel?"

"I love it so much, I wish we were on our way to get married."

"A week from today I'll be able to call you Signora Torriani."

Together they flew to Glarus under darkened skies. After landing, they called for a taxi to take them to the hospital.

Hasper's mother met them in the main lounge. The doctor joined them and they went up to the operating room where they were gowned and masked. The prosthetist came in and soon Hasper himself was wheeled in. His mother hurried toward him.

Luca and Bella waited before walking over to him. "We're here for you, Hasper."

"They said it won't hurt very much."

"That's because they've given you a local anesthetic. It will wear off and you'll have a new leg."

"Will you stay right here?" The boy's brown eyes beseeched him.

"I promise."

"You can bet your father loves you and is watching from heaven," Bella murmured.

Luca put his arm around her waist, loving

this marvelous woman beyond anything. She looked up at him before going over to sit by Hasper's mother and the procedure began.

Before long he'd been successfully fitted and was wheeled down to his hospital room, where they gathered round to celebrate. Bella presented him with a cell phone since he didn't have one. She programmed it with their numbers and his mother's. Luca showed him how to program the numbers of his friends.

At three that afternoon he and Bella left the hospital, excited for Hasper. He had a lot of rehabilitation to go through, but in time he'd be walking again. They took a taxi to the heliport. En route Bella had an idea.

"Luca? Since we're not in a hurry now, why don't we fly to Saint Moritz. Call your mother and tell her we'll be there for a while. I want to meet her."

"There's nothing I'd love more, but Dad will know and cause her grief."

"Not necessarily." He could hear her fascinating mind working. "You said she always grocery shops in the late afternoon. What store is it?"

"The Migros market."

"I know it's iffy, but could we rent a car and drive there? Maybe someone who works in produce or something could phone your mom and tell her about a sale that could get her over there right now. I want to get to know her. No doubt the spy network will inform your father, but not before the deed is done. He'll know it was our fault, not your mom's. What do you think?"

"You're brilliant, *bellissima*! I know the exact person."

Before long they arrived at the store and Luca introduced Signorina Cusso to Paulina, who ran the butcher shop.

"You're back in Saint Moritz already?"

His mother had been talking. Luca had an idea Paulina knew he'd moved to Scuol. Why not? They'd been friends for several decades. "Only for an hour. Would you do me a favor and call my mother? Tell her you've got a great sale on leg of lamb, my father's favorite. Tell her the deal won't last long so she'd better get over here now before it's all gone. Don't say anything else."

Paulina winked at him and made the

phone call. To his delight she hung up and said, "Your mother will be right over."

Luca paid her for a leg of lamb. "I've included a bonus for you, Paulina."

The woman wrapped it and handed it to him with a broad smile. "If you need privacy after she comes, just go out the back of the store through the produce section. You know where it is."

Indeed, he did.

Bella had been watching the byplay. "Maybe you're beginning to understand why I like living a normal life so much."

"You mean because I get away with murder?" he teased.

"In a way." Her playful smile was so alluring, it was a good thing they were surrounded by dozens of people. "While we're here, I'll do a little shopping so we can drive straight to the condo and eat."

"I'll help."

Ten minutes later they'd paid for a few items and Luca spotted his mother at the meat counter. "Surprise, Mamma." He put his arm around her shoulders and kissed her cheek.

"Oh, Luca—" she cried in joyous surprise.

"Come out the back of the store with me. Your leg of lamb is there waiting with someone I've been dying for you to meet for years."

"You mean Bella," she whispered.

They hurried through the produce area and out the door. Both women took one look at each other and hugged. For Luca it was one of the happiest moments of his life to see his two favorite women laughing and crying together.

He stood outside their circle while they got to know each other and communicated like mad. But after fifteen minutes, he tapped on his mother's arm. "I'm afraid if you stay here much longer, Papa will wonder what is keeping you."

She hugged Luca again. "Let him wonder. I'm getting to know my soon-to-be daughter-in-law. It should have happened years ago!"

"You're right, but now for your own sake, you *have* to leave." He pulled the wrapped meat from the sack and handed it to her. "Let's go back inside." With another kiss and hug, he and Bella watched her hurry through the store to the entrance.

He turned to Bella, whose beautiful face glistened with tears. Her violet eyes lifted to his. "She's so wonderful, I can't begin to tell you."

"You don't have to. It's written all over both of you."

"That's because we both love you so much."

After the drive home to Scuol, Bella fixed them a pasta meal he loved. But after one glass of wine, he got up from the table to kiss her. "I'm leaving now for the condo and you know why. We'll talk later tonight. Thank you for the delicious dinner and just being you."

Their marriage needed to happen soon or he wouldn't be able to honor his own rule. She knew it too and didn't fight him when he headed for the door. But before he opened it, Bella received a phone call from her brother. She put it on speaker.

"Vincenzo?"

"Where have you been, Bella?"

"In Glarus. One of the children the charity has helped was just operated on to fit a prosthetic leg. Luca and I just got back to my apartment."

"That's amazing what you're doing, but I have distressing news. Nonna Cusso might not make it this time. She's back in intensive care." Luca hugged her tighter. "The doctor says it's bad. Mamma left for Innsbruck and took the jet to Sardinia. Until we know more, Francesca and I are staying at the palace tonight to be with the grandparents."

Bella gripped her phone tighter. "I'm thankful you're there. Luca and I will drive over to the palace in a few minutes and we'll talk. Thanks for letting us know."

She hung up in tears. "Oh, Luca, I know it's coming, but you're never ready."

"At her age pneumonia can play havoc. I'm so sorry."

They cleared the dishes quickly, then left for the palace. "We can leave for Sardinia first thing in the morning, or even sooner if we have to, *bellissima*."

She nodded. "I should have stayed with her."

"But you didn't know she would have a relapse, and Hasper was counting on you. Surely you realize that because of your charity work, you were able to give him a new leg and pay for all the help he'll need. Did you see the love in his mother's eyes when she thanked you, Bella? None of this could have happened without you."

Her gaze met his. "I saw the love in Hasper's eyes when he asked if you would stay right there with him during the operation. You'll be his idol forever."

"I think his father holds that title. Today I couldn't help but imagine our own children one day."

"I thought the same thing. To have a family of our own would mean everything, but right now I'm so worried about Nonna."

"Let's not anticipate the worst." Except that being a doctor, he didn't have great hope she'd pull out of it this time. Her grandmother shouldn't have left the hospital the first time.

Bella clung to his hand all the way back to the palace. At close to nine they arrived and hurried inside. Vincenzo met them at the top of the stairs. "I'm glad you're here."

"I wouldn't be anywhere else." Bella hugged him.

Luca patted his shoulder. "I'm going back to the condo and get things ready in case we need to fly to Sardinia." He kissed Bella and hurried off so the two of them could be alone.

Bella turned to her brother. "In a way, I'm glad we're alone. I know a secret that you might or might not know. If you don't, it will blow your mind."

He held her upper arms and looked down at her. "What are you talking about?"

"Luca found out about it through his mother. What do you know about our great-great-grandfather Filipo Baldasseri?"

"That he was king and died from liver disease. His wife died from influenza. The Baldasseri line continued with our great-grandfather Alonzo, his son."

"What about his daughter Elsa?"

He thought for a minute. "She never married. She died of tuberculosis in a sanatorium hoping for a cure."

"You're telling me the whole truth?"

He frowned. "I swear it. What's going on?"

For the next few minutes she explained everything about Luca's great-grandfather and the awful tragedy that ended his career.

Vincenzo shook his head. "Poor Elsa, poor Basil."

"It's horrible, especially when the truth is that he tried to save her eyesight. It's the rea—"

"Oh, I get the reason," he broke in. "It explains the hate Luca's father has always felt for me."

"And me," Bella added. "Why do you think the King said his daughter had tuberculosis?"

"Probably because she needed care and a sanatorium would accomplish that," Luca reasoned. "Remember that his wife had died the year before."

"I can't bear to think about it. Elsa was blind and didn't belong in an institution. All she needed was love and attention."

"Let's face it, Bella. Our great-great-grandfather ended an honorable man's career out of anger because he needed someone to blame. Like you, I understand Dr. Torriani's rage against us and I'm going to look into it. Don't worry. Luca's mother needn't be concerned that secret can be traced back to her."

Bella hugged him. "Thank you, brother dear."

"Come on. Let's go in the drawing room until we hear from Mamma."

They walked inside and sat down. She pulled out her phone and sent Luca a text.

Darling? My brother knew nothing about Filipo and Elsa. He's horrified and will look into it without your mother ever knowing.

No sooner had she finished sending it than her brother got the call from their mother they all dreaded. At this point she phoned Luca, begging him to come back to the palace with his suitcase packed.

Luca arrived in lightning time and put his arm around her. "Tell me what happened, Vincenzo."

"Mamma spent the last few hours with her. They talked and suddenly Nonna didn't say anything more. The doctor rushed in, but she was gone. If it's any consolation, it was a very peaceful passing."

"I'm thankful for that," Luca murmured. "Do your grandparents know?"

"I just told them. They're in bed. The news was hard on both of them."

"Your poor mother. She shouldn't be alone."

"I agree and have made arrangements to fly us in the helicopter to Innsbruck in the next few minutes. We'll leave for Sardinia from there and help her plan the funeral. She wants it to be on Wednesday, four days from now. Francesca has to work Monday and Tuesday. Then she'll fly overnight to Cagliari with Rini and Luna. He loved Nonna too."

"We all loved her." Bella turned to Luca, and he caught her in his arms. Now came the hard part.

"Bella—I'm not going to the funeral with you."

Her face fell. "What do you mean?"

"This is one time when I refuse to intrude."

"But—"

"No *buts*." He kissed her lips. "We're not married yet. This is a family affair. I know your mother is grieving and I don't want my presence to disturb her while she mourns her mother. She'll want you and your brother at her side."

Her eyes filled with tears. "I can't bear the thought of going without you."

"Bellissima—I already had my chance to say my goodbyes to your *nonna* when we flew there. Once we're married, we'll do everything together, but now we need to do the right thing."

She clung to him. "I'm afraid."

He looked at her. "Why?"

"I don't know. I've got this terrible feeling something will go wrong."

"What could go wrong? A week from now we'll be married."

Fear broke out on her features. "What if there's some kind of surprise we hadn't counted on that prevents us?"

Luca hugged her tighter. "Nothing can prevent my marrying you. *Nothing.* Now come on. I'll help you out to the helicopter with your luggage. Let's hope you can get some rest on the flight."

"You think I could rest knowing we're going to be separated for the next five days and nights? I won't be seeing you until Thursday. Luca!" she cried in agony.

"Bella—what is it?"

"I'd die if we couldn't be together."

"We will be," he ground out, sucking

in his breath. "It's only five days, then no more separations ever."

"But you can't guarantee it."

"After ten years we found each other again. If that isn't a miracle, then I don't know what is. Believe in it. *I* do. I'll be here when you step out of the helicopter on Thursday and sweep you in my arms."

"What about your work?"

"I'll start my vacation on Thursday. We'll have ten days to honeymoon and do whatever we want."

"Do you have a place in mind?"

"I do, but I'll tell you after the ceremony."

She stared at him. "You have so much strength and faith."

"That's because your love gives me both. I'm the luckiest man alive. Now let's get you out to the helicopter, *mia amata*."

CHAPTER TEN

LATE WEDNESDAY NIGHT, Luca was just ready
to phone Bella when he received an unexpected call from Vincenzo.

"Hey, buddy. I'm surprised you're phon-
ing me now."

"This can't wait."

Luca got a sick feeling. "What's wrong?"

"It's fantastic news in the midst of this
sadness. I don't know how it will affect
your father, but it makes me love my great-
uncle Leonardo more than ever."

"What did *he* do?"

"As you know, my cousin Rini is like a
brother to me, the same way you are. I told
him about your mother's secret. He did a
lot of digging and a journal was discovered
with all Basil's notes regarding his operation on Elsa. The truth was there, proving

that he'd tried to restore her sight, but at the time King Filipo refused to listen.

"Rini was so appalled over the injustice done to Basil, he went straight to his grandfather with the journal. They pored over it together and the King actually wept when he had the proof in hand.

"He has already made a royal apology in front of the San Vitano parliament for the harm done to Dr. Basil Torriani and the entire Torriani family. He went further and sent letters to the medical society in Innsbruck explaining the miscarriage of justice. Lastly, he wrote a special letter of apology to your family in care of your father. It will be delivered to him by personal messenger from the King himself."

Luca sat on the side of his bed in absolute shock.

"Leonardo has also promised to make reparations to all living Torriani descendants for the damage done to your relative's reputation. I don't know if this will be enough to satisfy your father for all the hurt in your family, but it's a start in the right direction."

At the moment Luca was reeling. "A start

in the right direction? It's a miracle only *you* could have brought about. No man on earth ever had a better friend!" Overcome with this news, Luca had to fight tears.

After they hung up, he phoned Bella.

"I've been waiting for your call. I love you so much and can't wait to see you."

"It's a good thing our long wait is almost over. Right now I have something utterly incredible to tell you, *mia principessa*."

"You sound really excited. Tell me before I burst with curiosity."

"I have the most amazing news. But I'm trying to be sensitive because the grandmother you love has just passed away."

"I knew her death was coming. Our last phone call and all that coughing told me a lot I didn't want to admit. You sound different. Please tell me what's going on."

"You have a saint for a brother. I just got off the phone with him. He's done something I can never repay him for. He said that if I married his angel sister, that was all the payment he would ever want."

"He had to say that. Now tell me."

For the next little while Luca related what he'd learned from her brother. "I can't be-

lieve he called your cousin Rini to help
him uncover the truth about Basil. They're
both remarkable men I'm honored to call
my friends."

She broke down and had to clear her
throat. "Vincenzo has loved you all his life.
He'd do anything for you. I felt the same
way after I met you, and I love my great-
uncle Leonardo with all my heart for what
he's done. Rini's a saint too."

Luca nodded. "He's amazing. If my father can't overcome his hurt and anger after
all King Leonardo has done, then I don't
suppose there's any hope for him in that
regard."

"When we get back from Sardinia, you
and I can visit your parents and find out
your father's reaction."

"I'll see you tomorrow, Bella. I'm living for it."

CHAPTER ELEVEN

BELLA CLIMBED IN the limousine Thursday morning taking all of them to the airport. The funeral had been beautiful. Her mother had taken charge of Caderina's household. She'd handled everything with aristocratic grace and efficiency.

Both Bella and Vincenzo marveled at the way their mother was holding up. They knew her grief had to be unbearable without their father there to sustain her. They tried to help her, but she wanted to do everything herself. All they could do was stand by and offer comfort if she would let them.

When Rini had arrived with Luna and Francesca, their mother greeted them, but it was as if she were living in her own world, detached from everyone. Before long Bella got the feeling her mother wasn't living in reality. None of them could understand the change that seemed to have come over her.

Early Thursday Bella called Luca and told him her mother acted like a robot. "I don't know her like this, Luca. She stares at me with such a strange expression every time she looks at me."

"I'm sure your mother is in shock. She needs to get through all this before she can function normally. She'll recover soon and be herself," he consoled her.

"I'm sure you're right, but I've never seen her so…so unnatural."

"Give her time."

Bella had only been thinking of herself. "Luca—what about you? Did you tell your mother what the King has done?"

"Of course, and she's so overjoyed she can hardly talk."

"What about your father? I'm almost scared to ask."

"I'm driving to Saint Moritz now, but will return to Scuol at noon. Mamma said Papa received the couriered letter from the King yesterday and went into his office. She says he hasn't spoken about any of it. In fact, he's hardly speaking at all." A groan came out of Bella. "When he comes out for coffee, he walks around like he's in a daze."

"He didn't share any of it with her?"

"Not yet."

"No doubt that letter has sent him into shock."

"I'm surprised it didn't knock him unconscious."

"Oh, Luca—I can't wait until this is over and I can be with you. I need you desperately."

"Come home to me before the day is out, my love. Only a little while longer."

After they hung up, he made himself a bite to eat in the condo kitchen when the phone rang again. His mother's name came up on the caller ID. Now he could tell her he was driving to Saint Moritz.

He picked up. "Mamma? I'm just leaving to be with you."

"Thank heaven. I'm so glad you're coming, *figlio mio*. You must get here at once."

He'd never heard her this upset and his spirits plunged. "Are you ill?"

"No, but I'm going to be if your father doesn't come out of his office. He's been in there all night. He refuses to eat, won't talk, won't answer me, and the door is locked."

"I'm leaving now and will be there within the hour."

"Bless you."

Luca flew out of the condo and headed for Saint Moritz at top speed. The King of San Vitano had done everything in his power to make amends to their family for King Filipo's cruelty to Basil. Luca's father was a proud man, no doubt about it. But not to talk to his loving mother about this great blessing to their family really threw Luca.

As soon as he arrived at their house, he rushed inside where his mother waited for him in the living room. He hugged her, but could tell she'd been in pain. Together they walked through the house to his office.

"Papa? I just got here and I want to talk to you. Please open the door."

"Go away!" his father bellowed.

Luca had never heard him this out of control. He shared a worried glance with his mother.

"We need to talk, Papa."

"This is all your friend Vincenzo's doing! Damn him to hell and his interference! If you think this letter from King Leonardo changes anything, you're very much mistaken.

"How typical of this family to try and gloss over Basil's tragedy with meaningless words and money thrown at the problem. It's another case of the Baldasseris trying to force through what they want no matter what. Should you dare to marry Princess Baldasseri, your mother and I will disown you. Do you hear me? It will be as if you never existed on the face of this planet!"

His father sounded out of his mind for real.

Luca's mother grabbed his hand and shook her head. "There's no reasoning with him right now."

"I can see that. You're coming back to Scuol with me right now to spend the weekend. Grab the things you'll need and we'll leave."

"I can't, Luca. He's my husband."

She was noble and loyal to the end, but it would be her ruination to stay with him right now. "He has crossed a line, Mamma. Come with me and let him find out what it feels like to be without the love of his life."

"Oh, Luca. I can't believe this is happening."

His fists clenched. "I can, and now his behavior is hurting you."

"I shouldn't have called you."

"Oh, yes, you should have, and I'll always be here for you, Mamma."

"I know. I'm so sorry he's having such a difficult time accepting the inevitable."

Luca nodded. "A difficult time hardly describes his state of mind. It's clear he's going to take my marriage out on you if I go through with it." He walked around the living room for a few minutes, then stopped. "I can't allow that, not with you the sacrificial lamb for the rest of your life.

"I know Bella. She'll want you to live with us for the rest of our lives. We'll find a large place to live where you can have your own apartment. For a little while I believed we could make it all work, but now I know differently. Papa will have to live alone with what he's done."

"*Luca*—don't you think this will pass? Your father is a good man."

"I don't know. It may not be permanent, but I'm not letting his tantrum ruin everything. Go on and get packed. I'll help and we'll drive back in time to meet Bella's helicopter."

"But your father didn't used to be like this at all."

"That's true, but the situation has changed. I love you too much to watch him punish you because of my actions. He thinks he can stop this wedding, but he's going to find out differently."

An hour later they were ready to go. He walked through the house to his father's office once more and knocked on the door. "I'm leaving, Papa. Just so you know, Mamma is coming with me. Bella and I will be taking care of her from now on."

"I forbid it!" he yelled.

"Forbid all you want. If you only knew what a lucky man you really are. You married the woman of your dreams, a woman who's both saint and angel. She has loved you through all these years and put up with your anger and venom. Well, no longer."

They went out to the car with her luggage and left for Scuol. En route they stopped for groceries and a bite to eat. But they reached the condo much later than he'd anticipated.

After getting his mother settled, he texted Vincenzo to explain what was going on.

Dear friend, an emergency has come up. I'll explain later. I can't talk to Bella right now and won't be able to pick her up when you land in the next half hour. Keep her with you. I'll call her later.

"I don't see Luca's car," Bella whispered to Vincenzo after they all climbed out of the helicopter. Her mother had already gone inside the palace with Francesca.

Her brother put his arm around her. "Luca just texted me about an ongoing emergency. He said he'd call you in a little while."

"I just don't understand it."

"He's a doctor, remember?"

"I know, but—"

"Come on," he spoke over her. "Let's go inside. Mamma said she wants to have a talk with you. Since Luca can't come yet, now would be a good time."

Bella shook her head. "She wouldn't talk to me the whole time we were in Sardinia. *Now* she wants to talk? I can't take any more. After I go inside to change, I'm driving over to his office and wait for him."

She rushed inside the palace and hurried straight to her suite. After a quick shower and shampoo, she dried her hair and brushed it out, leaving it long. Then she put on her pleated white pants and a silky lavender blouse. Once she'd applied lipstick and slipped on her sandals, she was ready.

But when she whisked out the door, her mother stood there waiting for her with that strange look in her eyes.

"Mamma—I can't stay to talk, but I'll be back later."

Tears filled her mother's eyes. "You mustn't go until you've heard what I have to say."

Bella shook her head. "I've heard it all."

"No. You've never heard any of this. I only came to my senses in the last few hours before Mamma died. Let's go in your bedroom where we can be strictly alone."

What? "I can't right now. I have to find Luca."

"And I want you to. When you do find him, tell him that I'm no longer against your marriage. Luca *is* a wonderful man.

I've done a terrible thing trying to keep you from being with him. I thought I was being a good mother and guiding you to your destiny. Now I know that was wrong."

Something was seriously wrong with her mother.

"Mamma made me see things clearly for the first time in years. She spoke from her soul and told me how wrong I was to impose my will on you. She loved you so much, and she loved Luca. In him she saw all the attributes of a true prince. I was blinded by my own willful aspirations. Marcello went along with my wishes, but I know deep inside your father always approved of Luca and would want you two to marry."

All Bella could do was gasp.

"Mamma made me realize that I had no right to plan out your life. Being your mother didn't give me carte blanche to decide your path. Our long talk was an illuminating revelation that has made me see everything differently. More than anything in the world I want your marriage to take place in the church here."

"Y-you're serious—"

"Yes. I promised her that I would talk to Father Viret and ask him to marry you in front of our friends and family on Saturday. I called him before she took her last breath, and I've already spread the word so everything is set for your ceremony at ten a.m."

Bella stood there blinking in confusion. "What has happened to you, Mamma? I know Nonna's death has devastated you. But what you're talking about now doesn't make any sense. I simply don't understand you."

"Please believe me, darling. I'll be asking God's forgiveness forever after what I did to you following the avalanche. Luca has always made you the happiest girl on earth. I could see that, and resented it because it didn't go along with my rigid idea of what your life should be. I can only hope and pray that in the years to come, you'll forgive me and let me be a part of your life with Luca. Forgive me."

Bella broke down and embraced her mother. Joy filled her soul. She remembered Nonna's final words to her. *Everything is going to work out for you and Luca.* Bless her dear grandmother for her big heart and her wisdom. If Bella and Luca had a girl, they'd name her Caderina in honor of her.

Half an hour later, a shaken, overjoyed Bella left her mother in the bedroom and raced out of the palace for her car. She called Luca, but it went to his voice mail. In a panic, she drove to his office and rushed inside, only to learn he hadn't come in to work because of an emergency. When she called the hospital, they hadn't seen any sign of him either. Vincenzo swore he knew nothing except for the text Luca had sent him.

This meant that Bella's earlier premonition had come true. Something was horribly, horribly wrong. She rushed to the condo, but his car wasn't there, nor was he parked in front of her apartment. In a final moment of desperation, she phoned his mother in Saint Moritz. Again, all that greeted her was the call-forwarding message.

Not being able to find Luca took her back to the day when she'd tried to reach him after the avalanche and couldn't. This was a thousand times worse than déjà vu.

Bella got the feeling his disappearance

had everything to do with Luca's father. Instinct told her he'd gone to Saint Moritz to confront hm. This time Bella knew exactly where to find him. Together they'd face the bitter man who had the most marvelous son on earth.

Fifty minutes later she approached the door of the Torriani home in Saint Moritz. Luca's car wasn't around, but that didn't matter. She was here now and she would force him to tell her where his son had gone.

After knocking half a dozen times, the door opened and she faced the man who'd done so much damage to all their lives. "I'm looking for Luca. Do you know where he is? He was supposed to meet the helicopter earlier, but my brother received word there'd been an emergency. Have you any idea what that was about?"

He just stood there with his hand on the door handle looking dazed. In a way he reminded her of her mother while they'd been in Sardinia. "He was here hours ago. I have no idea where he is now."

"Is your wife here?"

His expression closed up. "No."

"I see. Well, just so you know, my mother

has had a change of heart. Luca and I will be married at the church on Saturday at ten by Father Viret. There's absolutely nothing you can do about it. Only you have the power to change the situation with your son. He's always loved you and always will.

"I'd like the chance to love you too. After all, you're the man along with your wife who gave him life and molded him into the sensational human being he's become. Any father on earth would give the world for a unique, marvelous son like him. How sad if you can't see what a blessing he is in all our lives. I'll love him forever."

Bella fought not to break down until she reached her car and headed back to Scuol. She'd go to his condo and wait for Luca. Then, as if it was a sign from the heavens, Bella's phone rang and Luca's face appeared on the call screen.

Luca had been watching for her from the window while his mother was getting comfortable in the guest room. The second he saw her car, he ran out of the condo and pulled her from the driver's seat. They threw their arms around each other, kissing each other hungrily. This long five-day wait had been the hardest of all.

"Forgive me for not being there when you flew in, Bella. I have so much to tell you. Mamma is inside with me. My father has turned into a madman, so she's going to be living with us from now on."

"That dear woman. I want her with us always. I knew something awful had happened between you and your father for you not to be there when we set down."

"Mamma called me early and told me to come to Saint Moritz quickly. I drove there as fast as I could. Papa wouldn't leave his office. He said the letter from King Leonardo meant nothing. He damned Vincenzo for his part in everything. Worse, he told me that if you and I married, he and my mother would disown me."

"Oh, no, Luca—"

"Oh, yes. I knew he'd take our marriage out on my mother since she'd given us her blessing. I had to have a long talk with her and convinced her to come with me. It took time to get her packed. By the time we reached Scuol, we weren't going to be able to meet the helicopter. I texted Vincenzo that there's been an emergency and that I'd explain later."

"I knew something ghastly had happened. When I couldn't find you anywhere, I drove to Saint Moritz."

"You're kidding—"

"I saw your father. He opened the door and he looked as dazed as my mother did back in Sardinia. He said he was alone. Now I know why. I gave him a piece of news that probably did blow him away completely."

He looked troubled. "What news?"

"My mother has undergone a total change of heart, all due to my *nonna* before she died." For the next few minutes Bella told him everything. "Mamma has begged my forgiveness and wants our marriage. She's a changed person, Luca. You won't believe it when you see her next."

"I think I'm having a heart attack, *bellissima.*"

"I know. I only wish the same transformation would happen to your father. I told him you loved him, and that I wanted to love him too. I told him we'd be married by Father Viret at the church on Saturday, just so he was informed."

Luca crushed her in his arms again, trying to take it all in. Bella's love for him washed over him like a giant ocean wave. "I've missed you so terribly that there were nights when I wanted—"

"To die?" she cut in. "Every night was like that for me. When you weren't there at the helicopter pad waiting for me, I knew my worst fear had been realized."

He grasped her shoulders and stared at her. "Your mother really has turned our world around. I'm out of my mind with joy."

"So am I, Luca. Maybe in time your father will have a change of heart too. But let's be thankful your mother is with us. I love her so much."

He threw his arm around her shoulders. "Let's go inside and discuss all our plans with her."

"You need to call Vincenzo too and ask him to be your best man. Tell him we'll never be able to thank him enough for everything he's done for us."

"I already did ages ago."

Once inside the condo, Bella looked

around. "We won't be married with the hares as witnesses after all."

"We'll go up there on our first anniversary. How does that sound?" He pulled her down on the couch and started kissing her, forgetting his mother, let alone forgetting that they weren't married yet. A long time passed before Luca lifted his head. "Two more nights and you're all mine."

Her smile illuminated his world. "I've been all yours since I was eight years old. How does it feel to be holding an ordinary girl in your arms?" she teased.

He traced the line of her lips with his index finger. "Princess or not, you were never ordinary, thank heaven. We'll never let it matter to our lives again."

"Amen, *caro*."

"Bella? Luca?" They both shot up at the sound of his mother's voice.

She laughed heartily. "Sorry to intrude."

Bella jumped and ran over to hug her. "You could never do that. I'm so thankful you're here. Luca has told me everything. Maybe your husband will have a change of heart in time."

"I'm wishing for that."

"Of course. We all are."

Luca walked over. "Bella drove to Saint Moritz looking for me, Mamma. Papa answered the door, still unreachable, but let's not allow that to ruin our happiness right now. Come in the living room and sit down."

It was like music to his ears as he listened while Bella told his mother of her mother's change of heart.

His mother laughed in a way he'd never heard her do before. "I'm elated and I can't wait to see you two get married on Saturday at the church."

"What about Papa?"

"What about him? While you were in here, I was in the guest bedroom talking to Bella's mother on the phone. Neither of us is worried. He'll either come around, or he won't. We both agreed men can be impossible."

Incredulous, Bella and he stared at each other before they burst into laughter.

"Wait—you've talked to Bella's mother?"

"Of course, Luca. Bella's bodyguard told her where we were and she called me, begging my forgiveness. I told her there was nothing to forgive. A mother tries to do the right thing for her child. In the end it is all working out. Both of us are looking forward to grandchildren. We agree you two can't get married soon enough. Do you have any other questions?"

CHAPTER TWELVE

THE REST OF Thursday and Friday were a scramble to get ready for the wedding. Bella called Constanza to be her bridesmaid along with Luna. Constanza would stay at the palace.

She asked her friend to come early to help her buy a wedding dress. It turned out to be a long silky white dress. No train and a short mantilla. Nothing a princess of the realm would wear. That was the way Bella wanted it.

Luca made calls to a few colleagues in Saint Moritz and Scuol to invite them to the wedding. Vincenzo went with him to buy a dress suit and take care of the flowers. On Saturday morning he drove Bella and his mother to the eighteenth-century church where both their families worshipped. The interior had been filled with flowers and scented candles.

To her joy, Rini and Luna arrived early. He'd been very close to Bella's father Marcello and planned to walk Bella down the aisle in his place.

As the church started to fill with family and church friends, Bella's grandparents arrived. The Visconti family flew in from Bern, including Francesca's brother, Rolf, and his fiancée, Gina.

Bella waited out in a room off the foyer in her wedding dress, delighted to see Francesca's boss, Dr. Zoller, and his wife enter the church. Two other people she worked with closely at the charity had also come. So far everyone she loved had arrived.

She kept watching and waiting. Only one person was missing. But she couldn't let it ruin this glorious day when she would become Luca's wife.

Vincenzo came in the little room at the last second with her bridal bouquet. "You're a vision, Bella. I hope Luca can handle your radiance."

She kissed his cheek. "I love you."

"The war has been a long one for you,

but it's over today and your new life of joy is beginning. If ever there were two people made for each other…"

"I feel the same about you and Francesca."

He squeezed her. "Rini is right outside."

"What a magnificent friend he's been." Her eyes filled. "Because of him, a terrible wrong has been righted."

"He's the best. So is Luca, but I don't have to tell you that."

"No. There's no one like him. If he hadn't become your best friend, I would never have known him. I can't even imagine it. Not to have known or been loved by Luca Torriani—" Her breath caught.

"Say no more. I understand completely." He kissed her cheek and left the room.

Bella picked up her bridal bouquet of roses and gardenias and walked out to join Rini. He looked every bit as dashing as Luca in a navy-colored dress suit.

"Dr. Torriani is one lucky man, cousin."

"I'm the lucky one to be walked down the aisle by you. The great service you have done to restore Basil Torriani's reputation will never be forgotten by me or Luca. My father loved you. More than ever I understand why. Thank you from the bottom of my heart for standing in for him today."

"It's my greatest pleasure, Bella. You were always more like a sister to me than a cousin. Are you ready?"

"The truth is, I've been ready for years."

He flashed her a beautiful smile. "The organ music has started. Let's go."

But before she could take hold of his arm, another person entered the church. A man. She took one look at him and almost fainted.

It was Luca's father!

He'd come! Luca wouldn't believe it. She could hardly believe it and looked up at Rini. "Do you know who that was?"

Rini smiled. "Oh, yes. It seems the miracle we wanted just came true. After you, Bella."

She took his arm and they walked through the foyer into the church. Bella felt as if she were floating in a dream. Luca stood near the altar with Vincenzo next to him. Her beloved wore a gorgeous dark blue suit with a gardenia in the lapel.

If a person could die from loving some-one too much, she was the prime candidate for all time. His eyes had focused on his father, who'd walked up to the front and sat next to Luca's mother. She'd been seated with Bella's mother, who sat next to her parents, Alfredo and Talia. *Incredible.*

This was a day out of time like no other. A miracle *had* happened. Her heart was bursting with joy. She could only imagine Luca's.

When she could gather her wits, she saw Luna and Constanza standing on the other side of the altar in beautiful ivory-colored gowns. Father Viret stood in the middle in his ceremonial robes.

Rini led her to the priest, who smiled at her. They'd been friends for years.

"What a beautiful sight," he began. "Two choice spirits who've worshipped here since they were born, wanting to be united in marriage. Two exceptional human beings whose love has brought them to God's house. Two sets of remarkable families all united as one on this glorious day."

Bella felt like this just couldn't be happening.

"Luca? Come and take Bella's hand."

Her gaze fused with his incredible green eyes for this first time since entering the church. She saw a light in them that had taken away the last shadow. To realize his father had come around had made all the difference in the marriage they were going to have.

Father Viret nodded to Constanza, who relieved Bella of her bouquet. Luca gripped her hand and held it fast.

"You two beloved people don't need a sermon in constancy or devotion. Others could learn from your example of how to love and never give up hope. Having said that, I'd like to marry you as soon as possible since I know you can't wait any longer."

She loved Father Viret.

"Bella Baldasseri? Do you take this man, Luca Torriani, to be your husband, to honor him, to keep him in sickness and in health, to love him with all your might, mind and strength?"

"I do!" she cried.

"And you, Luca? Do you take this woman to be your wife, to honor her and protect her, to keep her in sickness and in health, to love her with all your might, mind and strength?"

"I do and I will love her through all eternity."

"Then by the power invested in me by the

Church, I now pronounce you husband and wife. You may kiss your beautiful bride, Luca."

"Bellissima," he cried softly before covering her mouth with a husband's kiss. There was something different about it from all his other kisses. It was like a promise of things to come that sent sparks of desire through her entire body.

After he let her go, Father Viret said, "The congregation may congratulate Dr. and Mrs. Torriani out on the lawn in front of the church."

Suddenly the bells of the church rang for the whole town to hear. Luca hurried down the aisle with her. They reached the outside first. He kissed her again, almost taking her breath away. "I'm glad we're not having a reception. I need to be alone with you."

"You know I feel the same way. Where are we going?"

"To your brother's chalet in the mountains."

"Are you serious?"

"We'll stay there overnight before we do anything else. I can't handle the thought of being in flight twelve hours."

"I never wanted to go anywhere. All I

want is to be alone with you as soon as possible." She rose up to kiss his mouth once more and heard a deep voice say, "Luca? Bella?"

She turned her head and stared straight into the eyes of his father. His were a darker green and piercing. "I don't expect either of you to ever forgive me for what I've said and done."

"It's forgiven, Dr. Torriani," she cried. "You've come. It's the greatest blessing we could have. We'll never talk about it again."

Tears filled his eyes. "You mean it?"

"She means it," Luca spoke in a tear-filled voice. "Thank God you're here, Papa."

Bella watched father and son hug while she embraced Luca's mother, who said, "I prayed he'd come around. It just takes him more time than some people."

"Oh, I love you," Bella whispered. "Bless you forever."

Soon Bella's mother came over. "This was always meant to be, but I couldn't see it. Forgive me, darling."

"You couldn't help anything, Mamma. You've been such a wonderful mother to me. I can't wait until I have a baby who will fall in love with you."

"It would be my greatest joy."

They kissed before everyone else came over. After dozens of hugs, Luca told the crowd he and Bella had to leave.

Everyone laughed, especially Father Viret, who watched from a distance with Father Denis. He knew both their hearts and had done everything in his power to make the nonroyal ceremony short and sweet.

Twilight had fallen over the mountains. Luca hadn't noticed the time. His honeymoon had started eight hours ago. He'd made love to his wife all day and could have gone on all night. But it wasn't fair to her since she needed to eat. So did he when he thought about it.

Francesca and Vincenzo had done everything to supply them with food and comfort. They wanted for nothing. While she slept for a few minutes, he slid out of bed and threw on a robe. Before long he'd brought her dinner and put it on a table near them.

Could there be anyone more delectable than his new wife? Her long wavy hair swirled around her on the pillow. His eyes played over her body partially covered by the sheet, a miracle of feminine beauty. He was thankful he'd managed to remain true to his promise. Their wedding night was sheer rapture and worth the long wait. She gave and gave, filling him, completing him, with her love over and over again. If a baby resulted, nothing would make him happier.

Suddenly she opened her eyes and rose up on one elbow. "Where did you go?"

"I brought our dinner. May I serve you?"

"Oh, Luca. Yes." She sat up straighter.

He brought the tray over to the bed and got in, placing it between them. "Francesca takes the honors for our meal."

"My favorite, chicken scampi. Vincenzo must have told her."

"I love it too."

They ate while smiling into each other's eyes. "Could you believe Father Viret? He performed a quick, modern, commoner ceremony."

Luca drank some wine. "He loved doing it, you could tell."

She sipped her wine. "I saw your father

come in the church while I was waiting with Rini. I came close to fainting."

"So did I when he walked down the aisle." They continued to eat. "Mother had a lot more faith in him than I did."

"That's because their love is true and she knows him inside and out."

"The way you know me." He leaned over to kiss her cheek.

"Did it really surprise you when I phoned you the day after Vincenzo's wedding?"

"Yes. I wanted you to. I prayed for it, but after ten years… Since then I've learned a lot more about you. When you proposed to me in the tent and told me you'd given up your title, I began to hope that your love was here to stay forever."

"It is, and I want you to love me all over again, day and night. Do we have to go anywhere else on our honeymoon?"

"Not if you'd rather stay here."

"You know I do. But how do you feel? Tell me honestly, Luca."

"I've been waiting for you to beg me to stay right here until we have to go home." He moved the tray to the table and got back in bed, half covering her with his body.

"I'm addicted to you, my wife—every part of you. *Ti amo!*" he cried.

Luca devoured her with his mouth and rolled her on top of him. He needed to feel her arms and legs around him again, enclosing him as they once again began the age-old ritual that sent them soaring as one.

The hours passed. "You're so beautiful, no words can describe you. Love me, Bella. Always love me. I'm nothing without you." He covered her face and throat with kisses. "These past weeks of waiting came close to driving me mad. I've always had to love you from afar. But now we're married for eternity, and I can worship you with my body until the end of time."

"I love *your* body, Luca Torriani. I love your heart, your mind. Out of all the women in the world, I'm the most blessed one of all to be your wife."

He kissed her hungrily. "You're my very soul, Bella."

* * * * *

If you enjoyed this story,
check out these other great reads
from Rebecca Winters

The Greek's Secret Heir
Unmasking the Secret Prince
Reclaiming the Prince's Heart
Falling for the Baldasseri Prince

All available now!